BARE

An erotic novel based on true
stories.

Dash

Dash

Dash

BARE

Dash

TABLE OF CONTENTS

INTRODUCTION

Hi there,

Some of you may know exactly who I am and some of you may not. Either way, I owe you an introduction. My name is Mama Chunks, Big Mama if you're nasty! I'm a 30-year-old celebrity master masseuse, entrepreneur, and owner of Pure Intimacy. I have over 8 years of experience in massage therapy, but I've been perusing sensual massage therapy for four years.

I got into this work straight out of the military, Army, and I've been traveling the world servicing some of your favorite players, actors and of course, my everyday clients. I was medically separated from the military and knew that I couldn't just sit around collecting disability. Although that may float some peoples boat, it doesn't float mine. I wanted to do something that I knew I'd be great at and passionate about, so I started selling lingerie and sex toys. For some time, I didn't know how to express my sensuality and femininity so selling adult items helped fill that void. I began to ask myself "What else are you good at?" Selling the products was good but I wanted more. I thought back and remembered that I had knowledge in body work being that I went to school and graduated with my license in massage therapy, so why not massage in the same lingerie that I'm selling?!

That was a brilliant idea. Immediately, I purchased a massaged table, made some flyers of the services I'd offer, and posted them all over social media. The flyers garnered a bit of attention that helped me get some clients but not many. I had about 4-5 male clients that were on rotation throughout the month. It wasn't enough income for me, so I picked up a full-time job as a security officer.

It wasn't until one of those clients asked me to massage a woman he was dating. I had never sensually massaged a woman before, but I wasn't going to back down from the challenge. I agreed and he sent me the details. Now keep in mind, when I first started massaging, I was going into my clients homes or spaces that they reserved for this intimate encounter. I pulled up to the hotel and as I entered, a woman ran up behind me to catch the elevator. We greeted each other and headed up to the room. Neither of us knew that we were going to the same hotel room, I just knew that I was going to give a massage and she knew that she'd be receiving one. When we finally reached the door of the room, we giggled and entered.

After my client formally introduced us, I got to work. I massaged her like I would massage anyone else, but I took my time with her. As women, we require a bit more attention and care. I started by relaxing her body and made sure not to miss an inch. I caressed her gently and her body responded in ways that a man's body, cant. I got to her yoni and if you forgot, this was my first time ever giving a yoni massage, professionally. I used my fingers and massaged every crease. I transitioned to her clit and as she let out a very soft moan, my clit began to throb. I was familiar with how my body reacted with men during a session but with a woman?? Now I dated women so yes, they turned me on but in this space? How do I stay professional?? I refocused my energy by closing my eyes and allowing the music to speak to me. I took her on a journey just as the music took me on a journey. You would've thought I was a DJ the way I used my thumb to massage her clit. I didn't penetrate her in anyway, just strictly clitoral stimulation. Her moans were driving me mad. I reached back and picked up the bullet vibrator I had previously sat on the table behind me. I sat it on her clit while my other hand caressed her legs, feet, up to her breast then around her neck. She came so hard; I could feel her juices soaking the table. I didn't stop though, I kept going. She was screaming out yes and my client was sitting across the room jerking his dick. Boy was I in heaven. In that moment, I wasn't 100% sure how a complete stranger trusted me with her body the way she did, but she was enjoying herself and I wasn't going to ruin the moment. He came over, stood at the head of the table, and began caressing her breast. I didn't want to overstimulate her, so I lifted the vibrator off her clit to allow her breath to catch up. I know this is supposed to be about me, but I have to give you the backstory on how I got to writing this book so, sit back and enjoy the ride!

His hands brought her to a climax that was unknown to her, nipple stimulation. He twisted her nipples between his thumb and index finger. Gently, he plucked them, licked them, nibbled on them. "ME

NEXT!" I thought. I adjusted myself on the massage table to where I'm now laying between her legs. She had a blindfold on so she had no idea what would happen next or who was where. I used one hand to spread her lips while the other rubbed on her clit until she came again. My table was now soaked. I didn't come here expecting any of this to happen, I just came here to massage and go about my business. I sealed her massage by asking her to take three deep breaths. She climbed off the table and rushed to the restroom.

I began cleaning my table off while my client striked up a conversation.

"Wow Dash. That was intense! Thank you so much for doing this for me!" He said.
I thanked him for booking me and once the lovely young lady emerged from the restroom, the room fell quiet.

"How did you enjoy your massage?" I questioned, breaking the silence.
"I'll be 40 years old in a couple days and never in my life have I ever squirted. I've never had an orgasm like that before. Thank you so much! I needed that."

I continued cleaning but it wasn't until I flipped my table over to fold it up that I realized the amount of damage that had been done. My table was soaked through to the bottom and all over the carpet! I giggled to myself because GODDAMN DASH! Here I am anxious because this was the first woman I've ever given a sensual massage to a woman, and I made her drench my table??

Yep, we're taking this show on the road!! I packed up my things and left.

Later that evening, I went on twitter to tweet to my 600 something followers to how the service went and what happened. I included a photo of the bottom of my table, and of course, her identity remained private. When I tell you just from ONE retweet, my post went viral, that's exactly what I mean. I couldn't respond, all I could do was scroll. My comments were moving 100 miles per second, and I could not keep up. I was at work while it was happening and trying to stay focused on securing the property, just wasn't possible! I went from 600 followers to over 60k in the blink of an eye. My page was getting thousands of views across all of my platforms to the point all of my social media pages between Instagram and twitter, were hacked or disabled. There were a shit ton of negative comments, LMT's telling me that I give them a bad look, people calling me a prostitute and a bunch of other bullshit. The positive comments outweighed the negative ones, though. There were a lot of women telling me that they wanted the same treatment, they need intimacy, and asking how they can book me. I rushed to update my website and create booking links because I couldn't miss out on this! I wanted to ride the wave for as long as I could so, I hit the ground running. I scheduled a world tour going to 30 cities and I was in complete shock when I saw I was completely booked with 8-12 clients per city.

Here I am, a few years later and just completed my 7th and final massage tour. There's no way I could've made that long story short, so I hope you enjoyed it. In four years, I've massaged over 1,000 people, just little ol' me. I officially retired November 11th, 2023, and currently, drifting off into other world's to dominate them. From my success, I've created my own merch line that includes lingerie for women, apparel, colognes, perfumes, and a host of other products. I may have retired but please don't think it's the end of Pure Intimacy! We're still riding the wave baby. Plus, who's going to take care of my every day and high-profile clientele like Mama Chunks herself?

I wanted to write this book because I always tell my stories and always put y'all in my business, so why not have all of them or SOME, in one place? You don't have to go scrolling, looking for my story time, you can pour a glass of wine, dim the lights, and read this erotic novel based on all true stories, with your favorite vibrator nearby. If I make your pussy throb or your dick jump, my job I done. Enjoy these short stories as my gift to you!

Xo, Dash <3

Dash

CASPER

By the end of this chapter, you'll know exactly why his name is "Casper" and every time you read it, you may laugh but BARE with me... I met Casper while I was on my 6th massage tour early part of 2023. I typically have all clients send me a photo of themselves so that I would know exactly who I'm massaging. Now I've massaged some beautiful women and handsome ass men but Casper?? Casper was my EXACT type and baby I just knew it would be difficult staying professional with him. Casper was my last client of the day while in Jersey. I was finishing up with my client before him and this particular client, we'll call him John, was trying to linger. He wanted to hug and sway back and forth and shit. I did it because I needed attention, male attention. I was on my period and in that moment, I was craving a man's touch.

"Why don't you let me come back and show you a good time tonight." John whispered in my ear.

"Uhm, sir.. please just go. I have a client that'll be here soon and I'd much rather him show me a good time." Is what I said in my head, but John was big as hell. He stood at 6'5 with humongous ass muscles and being embraced by him just felt, good. Safe. So, although I was thinking I wanted him to leave, and although I wanted him to leave, my body didn't.

"I'm on my period and I really just want to relax. I'm not going to be in the mood to entertain tonight." I said.

That didn't seem to bother him not one bit.

"That's fine with me" John countered. "We can just cuddle and lay up.

I dislike when a man try to push himself onto me, but I wasn't opposed to the idea. Jersey was my second to last city and I'd been to 21 cities prior to Jersey. A little affection wouldn't hurt, would it??? I finally agreed to let him come back later that evening and now it was time for me to push him out the door to prepare for Casper's appointment.

Ding My phone alerted me to a text message which of course was Casper. I sent him the instructions and waited for him to get to the room. There were rose petals everywhere, candles lit, soft, relaxation music playing and the aroma in the room was just right. Sensual massages are foreplay so of course the mood has to be set the moment the door swings open. I stood at the door of my hotel room looking out the peephole. Even though I keep myself safe while doing this work, I don't have time for funny business so watching out the peephole, was a necessary step. I saw Casper approaching the door, so I slowly began to open it.

"Hi there!" I exclaimed. "Welcome in. How are you?" Casper was even finer in person, goddamn! He had gorgeous brown almond slanted eyes, stood at about 5'7, chocolate with a very well-tailored beard and a low cut with the deep waves. He was dressed in all black, no jewelry and a smile that he wore ever so graciously.
"I'm good, beautiful, how are you?" He asked.
His voice was deep yet soft with a heavy New York accent. "I'm great, thank you! Thank you for also being on time!" I joked. I went straight into my disclaimer and when I mentioned I'll be wearing gloves when I got to his lingam massage, he chuckled. "What's funny?" I asked.
"Oh nothing. You have to protect yourself and I respect that." "Are you ready to begin?" I questioned him.

"I am." He said. That was the last of the talking between us until...

Casper climbed on the table while I turned on my playlist and I went to work. I was highly attracted to him, so I did a little extra during his massage. A bit more pressure here, my titty in his mouth there. Nothing too crazy. You're probably wondering "Is she giving him a nuru massage?" No, I wasn't. I had on black silk booty shorts with lace trimming and a lace bralette that my DD's seemed to escape from with every movement. I wasn't in a rush to tuck them away, though. Now with my disclaimer, I do ask for consent so don't think I'm out here stuffing my titties in people mouth! I finally get to his lingam massage, and I glove up. I started massaging his penis and yes, it's big but it's soft. I'm used to having to put the work in to get it hard, but his dick wasn't budging. It stayed soft!

"Am I losing my touch?" "Is he not enjoying his massage?" "Is he uncomfortable?" All of these questions plus more, flooded my mind until Montel Jordan x What's on Tonight, blasted through the speaker interrupting my thoughts. It was the song that let me know the massage was coming to an end and we needed to wrap it up. I climbed off the table, walked to the head of the table, and sealed the massage by asking him to take three deep breaths.

I hurried off to the restroom to wash my hands and as I returned, Casper was almost fully dressed. The thoughts from before immediately popped back into my head.

"Did you enjoy your massage?" I asked him. "Are you a bit more relaxed than you were before you came?"

"I definitely enjoyed myself. The massage was amazing. I would book you again in a heartbeat if you come back to Jersey." He responded.

Contrary to what his mouth was saying, his body didn't give me anything. Not a moan or a groan or any indication that he was relaxed. Of course, I still went through the motions of it because well, he paid me. We talked briefly while he continued getting dressed then we said our goodbyes. I cleaned up my massage table and before I could finish, my phone alerted me to a text.

"I really did enjoy my massage. I'd love to take you to dinner if you'd let me."

It was Casper!!! Sir! Hell, yes you can take me to dinner, but I had to play coy.

"That's really sweet of you. Thank you but you don't have to do that." I replied.

I had mentioned that I was hungry and was going to head out to find food after I freshened up. For him to offer was really kind. I try not to blur the lines between business and personal, but I don't report to anyone but myself so... hey!

"I know I don't have to. If you're blowing me off, just say that." He shot back.

What is it with these jersey men? They don't take an indirect no for an answer. Or maybe, just maybe, they could smell the pheromones radiating off my body that told them I NEEDED male attention? At this moment, I didn't care. Fuck it. YOLO! I picked up my phone and responded to him.

"If you can give me a moment to shower, I will go to dinner with you."

I dropped the Clorox wipes in the trash and headed straight for the shower. Stepping out, I oiled myself up with my Vanilla Body Oil and sprayed my Signature perfume, both by Pure Intimacy, and got dressed. I slipped into a chocolate brown maxi dress, grabbed my jean jacket, and hurried down to the hotel lobby. As I walked out of the hotel, Casper got out of the Tesla doubled parked in the driveway and opened my door. Before grabbing my hand and leading me to the car, he gave me a long hug. The one where his hands are planted on my lower back but also resting on my ass with my arms thrown over his shoulders? Yes, that kind of hug. You would've thought that we'd known each other longer than an hour. He escorted me to the car, closed my door and we headed to the restaurant. We pulled up to Bonefish Grill and although I had never been there before, they apparently had exactly what I wanted, salmon and veggies. We were seated and Casper immediately sat next to me in the booth.

"What was the best part of your massage?" I asked him. "When you were massaging my shoulders and chest, singing in my ear." He replied. "I wanted to touch you, to feel you, but I wasn't sure if it was allowed."
Now here I am, all in my head thinking he didn't enjoy his massage when in reality, he was just taking it all in and being respectful to my boundaries.
"I also enjoyed you massaging my dick, and had you not had on gloves, I would've been hard as a fucking rock." He said.
"So, you're a skin-to-skin kind of guy?" I questioned.
"I am but again, I respect you and what you do so I wasn't going to ask you to take them off."
"So how about... I give you round two. Tomorrow?" I suggested.
It was a win-win for both of us. He'd get the release he needed, and I'd get, well... to give him that release. Casper agreed to come back tomorrow morning before I checked out to get his round two. We talked some more, laughed, touched, picked off each other's plate. It was cute. A cute little date ducked off in the back of the restaurant. The entire time I was with

him, my phone would NOT stop vibrating. I mean calls and texts. I didn't want to be rude by picking up my phone so when Casper excused himself to the restroom, I checked it. It was John, my client from earlier in the day. I told him that I had went out for dinner and that I'd be back at the hotel soon.

Me and Casper finished dinner and he took me back to my hotel. He once again, opened my door, kissed me, and hugged me goodnight.
"I'll see you in the morning beautiful."
"I'll see you in the morning." I replied. "Goodnight" I turned to walk into the hotel and the minute the doors opened, John was sitting right there, watching! My heart sunk! I felt like had just got caught doing something that I wasn't supposed to be doing. I walked up to him.
"Hi! Are you ready?" I asked. He stood up and we walked to the elevators in silence.
"How was your dinner?" He questioned.
I wanted to laugh, knowing that I just had one of the best dates I'd had in a while, left that date to come and cuddle up with someone else.
"It was good. I enjoyed myself."
We finally made it to the room after a silent elevator ride and I headed straight for the shower. Me and John cuddled up and relaxed. That was until he... well, you can't get that part of the story just yet. Keep reading and you'll find out what happened with us.

Casper came the next morning as planned. I gave my disclaimer as I usually do and got to work. I went through all the same motions but of course added a bit extra because, you know. This time was different though. Casper's hands were all over my body. He didn't leave an inch untouched, and I loved every second of it. The songs on my playlist tell me where I should be in the massage, and I felt time was just moving too damn fast. Normally, it's my client not wanting the massage to end but this time, it was me. It was time for the moment of truth. The time when I got to wrap my soft pretty hands around that big dick of his. I grazed his dick with my fingertips, and it jumped. GIRL IT JUMPED! I just knew I was about to tease him better than I had ever teased anyone before. I got to going. Stroking it, massaging it, spanking it, softly. His moans were deep. I picked up my rhythm then slowed it down. He was right. His dick was hard as a rock. I wanted nothing more than to sit on it, but I couldn't. I mean, I could've but you never know who's into running red lights. Maybe I was teasing myself more than I was teasing him. I jerked his dick to the music, slow, fast, slow fast. He finally erupted all over my hands and his nut was so pretty. Very healthy and smooth. I rushed to the restroom to quickly wash my hands and came back to seal his massage with deep breaths. Unlike yesterday, he laid on my table for a moment trying to gather himself. He didn't immediately rush to get dressed, he just laid there.

"How was your massage?" I asked with a smirk.

"Wow."

That's all he could say. No other words just, wow.

Me and Casper communicated for a month after and I asked if he'd like to be my muse in a promo video that I was shooting. He agreed and we decided to meet in Philly to shoot. The day flew by, and all I could think about was seeing his face again. I went down to the bar of the hotel to have a few drinks until Casper and my team arrived. I was still at the bar when he got there and baby, the man looked so fucking good. So good, that I wanted to eat him alive right there! We went to the room, and I introduced him to my videographer and creative consultant. We immediately got to work. We worked for about six hours straight and I must admit, it felt amazing just having him there watching me. When we finally wrapped, all I wanted was to cuddle up with Cas and sleep.

Casper walked my team out to their car and came back to run me a shower.

"It's just you and me now." He said, kissing me.
"Just you and me." I whispered.
We stepped into the shower together and unexpectedly, he began to wash me. Every inch of my body was covered in soap. It was one of the most romantic things I had ever experienced. I stepped out to allow himself to shower and waited for him on the chaise to oil me up. We cuddled up in bed, kissing, touching, rubbing.
"Come here." He said, in between kisses.
I climbed on top of him, not missing a beat. His fingertips traced my spine as I straddled him, and my body gave completely into his touches. He talked to me through his kisses, affirming me and that alone, has to be top five of the sweetest things I have ever encountered. I kissed down his chest and made my way to his dick which was standing fully at attention. I took my time

kissing all 10 inches of that thick, chocolate, beautiful dick before I took him into my mouth. The room was dim, but I could still see him as I looked up and we locked eyes. I sucked his soul right out of his body. I watched his chest cave as he took deep breaths. I kissed the head. I licked the head. I sucked the head. Then, I swallowed him up. I wanted to suck his dick longer than he allowed me to. I had some tricks to show off, but Cas palmed both sides of my face pulling me up to kiss him. He flipped me over on my back, cupped my titties and started sucking my nipples. I mean he did it with such ease. He took his time. The sensations were driving me insane; I could feel my juices flowing down my ass crack! I wanted him deep inside of my pussy, but he didn't. Not yet at least. He kissed my pussy, teasing me the same way I had just teased his dick. He kissed my thighs, my lips. He kissed everywhere except my clit! I was yearning for it. I could feel him breathing on it, but he just rested between my legs. My body moved under him, begging him to please partake in his meal. Finally, he kissed my pearl, and I lost it. He ate. He feasted. He reached both hands under my ass and pulled me into his mouth. My body writhed under him. I cradled his head with one hand and massaged my nipple with the other. I looked down at him, trying to watch him eat but I couldn't focus. Casper had my entire body under his spell. It gave into him at every one of his commands. He didn't speak. Not one verbal word but my body listened to him.

"I'm cumming! Casper!!! I'm fucking cuming!"

I came so hard in his mouth, but he wouldn't stop eating. My legs were trembling, hell, my entire body

was trembling. He kissed back up my stomach until he reached my face. I gripped his face, massaging my juices into his beard while sucking on his tongue. "Open up." He said softly.
I spread my legs without hesitation. Cas slowly put his garden hose deep into my love garden and when I say slowly, I mean SLOWLY. He looked me in my eyes and said,

"It's okay, I got you. Daddy got you. Open up."
Immediately, I came, again. The way this man took his time with me, I almost told him I loved him! Now with every inch of dick deep inside of me, he left it there. He didn't move and neither did I. We caught each other's breath and stayed in that moment. I could feel my pussy gripping him and his dick pulsating in me. Casper lifted himself up and grabbed my ankles in each of his hands. He stroked me, then fucked me. Stroked, then fucked. When he'd feel me running from him, he'd follow me.
"I'm sorry baby. Don't run from me."
Immediately, I came. Again.
Every single time he opened his mouth to speak, I came. Over and over. In such a small period of time, he learned my body so well. He listened to me. He listened to my body. He knew what I could take and what I couldn't. When I thought I couldn't, he reassured me that I could and forced me to take it, consensually. Every position he put me in from doggy to cowgirl, he was in control. He told me what to do and I did it.
"You're such a good girl. Look at your fine ass taking all that dick."
Immediately... I came.

I rode his dick so good; it was hard for him to hold back his nut, but he did. I bounced my ass on him. He grabbed each cheek

and slammed me down onto him repeatedly. I was so proud of myself for taking it.

"That's right. Give that pussy to Daddy."

I locked my fingers behind his head, climbed up onto my feet and bounced my ass just on the tip of his dick. He could no longer hold out on me. When I knew he was about to cum, I pussy swallowed him up. I sat down on him and began grinding into him so his dick could glide across my A-spot. I wanted to take him for every drop of nut he had. We moaned loudly together as we reached our climax. I'm sure by now, the entire floor of guests heard me screaming out this man's name, but I didn't care. I collapsed onto his chest, hips hurting, knees hurting but that was the least of my worries. We had just made love to each other. I was in heaven I didn't want to come down. We spent the night cuddling, listening to music and of course, fucking.

I call him Casper because a couple months after our encounter, I reached out to him to send him the final project that he starred in only to discover I had been blocked. We had very little conversation from the time I left him in July to the time I reached out to him in September, so for me to be blocked was a huge surprise. I looked everywhere for this man, Facebook, Instagram, twitter, hell, I even uploaded his photo to google photos and still couldn't find him. Not a LinkedIn, a Myspace, black planet, NOTHING. Not because I was pressed for dick but more-so to understand why the hell I was blocked when we both understood each other's situation.

Cas finally contacted me in November because he was in North Carolina and wanted to see me. My first thought of

course, was to curse him out - which I did but you better believe that immediately after I cursed him out, that dick was in my throat. I mean love making so good that my waist beads popped, my nails broke and the feathers from the pillows, were all over the room.

Dash

NICK

Nick was some of the best sex I've had in my life. We have a long history so let's start at the beginning, shall we? I met Nick when I was 20 years old in 2015 at a church event. He stood in the door of the church, and you would've though I saw Jesus himself the way I had to do a triple take. I immediately knew I wanted him. Hell, physically, he was the type of man I had been dreaming about. From where I sat, I couldn't get his attention, so I knew I'd have to wait until service was over just to say hello. I excused myself to the restroom just before the alter call and as I re-entered the sanctuary, Nick was sitting on the stairs at the pulpit. Because the prayer was going forth, I couldn't walk through and return to my seat, so I stood there, right in front of him. I could feel him watching me, so I made sure not to look in his direction. I wore the classic black and white uniform that's worn during principal services; a white button up shirt, a black pencil skirt, black pantyhose with a pair of So Kate lookalike black stilettos. Of course, I had to make it edgy, so I added a black leather cropped jacket. I looked amazing. I was always the young woman in church that the older generation looked for every Sunday because they knew I was going to step.

Church was finally over, and I needed to charge my phone to call my mom to pick me up. Nick sat at the keyboard, and I figured that not only would there be an outlet nearby, but this would be the perfect opportunity to speak to him. I proceeded to walk in his direction.
"Is there an outlet behind you? My phone is completely dead, and I need to charge it." I said to him. He swiftly stood up and allowed me to sit on the bench for access to the outlet.
"Hi there, I'm Nick" he said extending his hand for me to shake. I extended my hand.
"My name is Cooki-, I'm sorry, my name is DaShawn, but my friends call me Dash. It's nice to meet you!" I stumbled on my words as I introduced myself. The man was fine as hell just staring into my eyes, holding my hand. I didn't know which name to tell him, the name I go by, my nickname or my real name. Embarrassment number 1. He chuckled and as we exchanged surface level conversation, my gitters went away. "So, what do you do, Nick?" I asked
"I'm a musician. How about you?"
"Well currently, I'm training to enlist into the Marines but I'm also in school for massage therapy while

working at the Horseshoe casino." I thought being so ambitious at such a young age was a flex. Out of all I said, all Nick heard was 'training for the Marines'.

"So that means I won't have much time with you, huh?" He inquired.

"I guess you'll have to take advantage of the time you have me with me then." I knew what my intention was and at that time I had no idea what I would be getting myself into.

Nick stepped outside, and I figured that when he came back inside, I'd ask for his number. I didn't have much time being that my ride was about five minutes away, so I walked outside, and he was nowhere in sight. I felt a small sense of defeat because, damn. One, where did he disappear to that quick and two, why did he leave without saying goodbye? Being that I was at my godfathers church, I knew one of my favorite members would have the scoop on him. I walked up to Jay and asked him for the 'car-fax'.

"You don't want him Cookie. I promise you he's not worth it." I didn't know what the hell that meant but since Jay wasn't going to hook me up, I for sure was going to do it myself.

When I got home, I pulled up Facebook and started doing some digging. I went to Jay's friend list as well was my godfathers. If Nick was a musician like he said and was well known throughout churches across the east coast, he'd for sure be on either of their pages. Bam! What do you know, he was there. I didn't waste any time. I sent a friend request and as soon as he accepted it, I sent a message.

"You left before I could say goodbye. It was really nice meeting you today! Have a great evening." I had to be subtle. Well shit, my thirst wasn't subtle at all. I swiped out of messenger and went to his page to scroll through his photos. Every picture was just as I remembered him from a few hours ago. Nick stood 6 feet tall, a clean-shaven head and a salt and pepper beard that sat perfectly trimmed on his gorgeous caramel skin. His light brown eyes were piercing. Perfect lips, perfect bone structure, everything. His style was immaculate. His suits were tailored to fit and if his clothes could talk, they'd tell you he was the perfect gentleman with a hint of rugged. I checked my notifications, and he still hadn't responded. I occupied my time and ultimately ended up going to bed.

A trip to the restroom woke me up in the middle of the night and naturally, I checked my phone to see the time. It was almost 1:30am and a message from Nick was awaiting me. I smiled and unlocked my phone.

"It was nice meeting you as well, beautiful. I was in a rush and couldn't come back to say goodbye, but I enjoyed chatting with you."
"So that means you owe me a hug whenever I see you again." I responded coyly.

"That wouldn't be a problem. Here's my number, use it when you're ready."
SCORREEEEEE!!! Did I really just bag this man that easy? Yes, yes I did. I didn't want to appear desperate, so I waited until the next day to text him.

While on the light rail heading to work, I texted him just so that he'd have my number as well and I wouldn't feel so pressured to be the only one reaching out. We texted for a short while until I got to work, but being that I was a cage cashier, I couldn't have my phone on the floor. I snuck my phone inside my drawer just to check throughout the day if he'd text me. To my surprise, he called! I faked a bathroom break just to call him back because, why not? It wasn't a long conversation, but I definitely turned on my sexy, seductive voice. That always gets them. He just wanted to check in on me being that I expressed how working at 7am in a casino was stressful as hell and I appreciated him for even calling to ask how I was doing.

For some time, me and Nick talked every day. It had been a while since I saw him last, and I thought there would be nothing better than being in his company, even more, his arms. Throughout our daily conversations, I would tell him how I liked it, how I wanted it and what I needed him to do to me. I had a huge obsession with BDSM from watching porn and with the way Nick dominated me just through text messages, I knew my fantasy could and would be fulfilled. We planned for me to come to his apartment the following week and God knows I couldn't wait. I counted down the days and had already purchased some sexy lingerie that I would wear for him.

The day had finally arrived, and I caught the MTA two and a half hours all the way to him. Yes, TWO HOURS! He was worth it, and I was just about to find out how much. As soon as he opened the door, he immediately grabbed me and pulled me into him. He closed the door, his lips never leaving mine. I dropped my book bag and wrapped my arms around him as tight as I could. I missed him. I wanted to be in his skin. We finally released each other and just stood there staring into each other's eyes. We relaxed on the couch for a moment until I asked if I could shower and get a little more comfortable. He agreed and in my mind, it was time.

I showered and layered some Pure Intimacy fragrances that I knew he'd love. I opened the door and walked out to him. I wore an all-nude thong body suit with nude thigh highs and matching heels. I sat on the sofa next to him with my legs crossed as I allowed the light from the TV to dance across my chocolate skin. The super bowl was on and instead of him watching the game, he was watching me. A sly smile crept across my face. Nick stood up, walked to the back of the apartment, and emerged holding his hands behind his back. "Get up." He demanded. "Why?" I asked.
"Dash, get up." This time, his voice was more stern. I stood up as I was instructed.

"Turn around." He said. I giggled as I turned my back to him but also making sure I followed each of his instructions. I didn't know what to expect but I quickly felt a cool piece of satin gliding across my eyes. As he tied the strings in the back, I remembered that we briefly discussed a fantasy where I wanted to be blindfolded. He took my hand and led me to the back of the apartment. I was so intrigued by what was happening, and I had so many questions. Nick wasn't the kind of man you questioned, so I kept quiet.

"Kneel." He ordered.

I did as I was told. I felt the hard, rough surface against my knees, but I didn't know exactly what I was kneeling on. I couldn't think of it being a single thing except wood. Where the hell did he get wood from??

"Spread your legs." Nick interrupted my thoughts and began to tie my ankles to the wood. I forced myself to hide my excitement. I felt him move around to the front of me.

"Open your mouth." I was met with a gag ball, and nothing could've prepared me for the spit that would immediately start to pool in my mouth.

"Ass up, face down, arms out." His demands were getting more and more serious, yet I followed each one to a T! I stretched my arms out and felt his hands in mine. He turned my hands so that my palms were facing upwards. I began to feel the same material I felt on my ankles, around my wrists. Rope. It was hard, kinda scratchy but sturdy. Although uncomfortable, he did place a pillow under my pregnant belly. We'll get that story another day. I was tied tight to this piece of wood. I couldn't move an inch even if I tried.

I already knew what Nick's dick looked like from the pictures and videos he had sent me but in person? I didn't know if I could handle it. WHAM! A hard, cord like rope came down hard on my ass. "Arrgghhh." My sounds were muffled.

Surely I wasn't expecting to get my ass whipped. I've seen floggers and whips, but I didn't think they felt like this. WHAM! He hit me again. Immediately tears began to well up in my eyes and fall. I couldn't move.

I couldn't go anywhere. This man had complete control over me. Although in pain, deep down, I was so turned on. He hit me a few more times until he started to speak.

"You like that?" His tone was slightly sinister.

I didn't respond because I honestly didn't know if I liked it, but I also couldn't because I had a gag in my mouth. He hit me again. "I said, do you like that?"

"YESSSS!" I moaned but still muffled.

He approached my body and ripped the crotch of my bodysuit in one swift motion. He plunged himself deep into me. No warning. No preparation. Just every inch of dick deep inside of me. I cried out in pleasure, spit dripping from the corners of my mouth.

"Damn this pussy is leaking." He mumbled.

I could feel my juices sliding down my leg every time he pulled out and thrusted himself back into me. Nick continued to fuck me, hard, until I was about to explode then he stopped. WHAT THE FUCK IS HE STOPPING FOR?? I needed this. I needed to cum. Before I could form another thought, Nick was using the same cordlike rope he used to whip my ass, to whip my palms. Now this was a different kind of pain. I twisted my wrists and balled my hands into a tight fist just to stop the pain, but he didn't stop hitting them. At this point, I was sobbing. The blindfold was soaked.

I was finally able to push the gag out of my mouth and scream in pain.

"Did I tell you to remove the gag Dash?" He was calm but serious.

"No, Papa." I whimpered.

"Open your mouth."

I opened my mouth but this time it wasn't the ball gag, it was his dick. He held the back of my head with one hand and his other held my chin; the perfect positioning to fit all of his dick in my mouth. He stroked my throat gently then aggressively and gently again. He bent down to kiss me and to remove the blindfold. He wiped my tears away and asked if I was okay.

"Yes Daddy. I want more, please."

"I knew you would."

His pearly white teeth glistened as he chuckled and returned to holding my face while fucking my throat. I couldn't tell the difference between my tears of pain and my tears of pleasure. Submitting to Nick came naturally for me just as him fucking me senseless came natural for him. He continued to violently fuck my throat and the more I tried to run, the more the rope loosened from around my ankles and wrists. I was finally free. Now, I had more access to him. I'm not sure if Nick noticed that the rope had come a loose as he was ravaging my throat, but I propped myself up on my hands and started to throw neck. It was my turn to rock his world. The switch in me piqued her head. 'FINISH HIM' is what I heard my subconscious say. Nick laid me back on the wooden surface and plunged himself into my pussy, again. With my ankles crossed and sitting on his shoulders, Nick put me out of my misery.

"Fuck me just like that." I moaned. I could feel his juicy dick massaging every wall inside of my pussy. I reached for the pillow that was once under my stomach and put it under my hips. I wanted to feel him deeper inside of me. I watched him as the beads of sweat dripped down his face. We locked eyes but not for long. Nick grabbed my hips, flipped me over and forced me once again, to arch my back. I spread my knees and held onto the wood. This is going to be a wild ride! I began to whine my hips slowly back into him.

"Ahhh fuck." He groaned.
Now you tell me if you can handle seeing my soft, supple, chocolate brown ass bouncing on your dick under the moonlight. I placed the pillow under my face, arched my back as deep as it could go and reached around to spread my ass so he can dig deeper into me. I used my waist and hips to counter every blow he gave me. Nick had the perfect angle to see my tight, wet, pretty pink pussy grip his thick dick. We caught each other's rhythm, and we rode the wave. When I felt him start to tense up, I started to massage just the tip of his dick with my pussy and tightened my muscles around it to swallow every drip he had to release then I slammed my ass back on him.
"Goddamnnnnn!" He screamed out.
"Yes Daddy. Give it to Mama." I whispered. As our motion slowed, I continued to stroke his dick. We stayed in that position for about 60 seconds, just feeling each other. Nick was still throbbing inside of me, and I was still tightening my pussy, keeping him in me. When I finally released him, he helped me up off the wood. To my surprise, it was a wooden palette that of which you'd see at Walmart. Where the fuck did this fool get a wooden palette from?? We headed for the bathroom to shower.

I winced in pain as the water cascaded over the areas the rope was just removed from. We looked at the bruises that now surfaced on my skin and Nick just held me. I needed that aftercare. The intimacy soothed me. I felt safe. He began to wash me ever so gently. He took his time with me. I'm sure he noticed how fragile I was from our encounter just a few moments ago. After cleaning us both, we emerged from the shower and went to rest on the sofa, both of us, completely naked. Nick propped my body up on his and we cuddled in silence. About 5 minutes later, he pulled out his phone.

"Guess what I have." His voice was low and sexy yet excited. Before I had the chance to answer, he pulled up his photos and casted a video to the tv. I couldn't believe it! He recorded the entire damn thing! From the moment we walked into the bedroom from the living room to the moment my pussy sucked him dry. The masterpiece was 48 minutes long and in the moment, it felt a lot longer than that. We ordered pizza and watched the video over and over.

"What was your favorite part?" I inquired.

"When I had you tied down and the first hit of your ass with the rope, your pussy immediately started leaking. That shit was beautiful to me. What was yours?"

"Honestly, the entire thing." I said. "It was more mental for me. Initially, I didn't know what was happening. I was a little scared, especially when you started whipping me. It was painful. There were a lot of thoughts running through my head, but I also trusted you. My body trusted you. Allowing myself to submit to your dominance was the best part and opened up other areas in me I didn't know existed." We continued through the evening chatting about the video, what our expectations were, him being the

Godfather to my baby and eating our pizza. Once we were done, I wanted to feel him in my throat, again. Everything I had just eaten came right back up on his dick, but he loved that nasty shit. Hell, I did too. I just didn't know it. We fucked all over the couch, the floor, bent over the bathroom sink, the dining table, the kitchen counters, everywhere except the bed. We couldn't get enough of each other. I longed for this. I wanted every part of him because who knew when we'd see each other again? We finally got into bed and held each other the entire night. No matter how much I tossed and turned, he never let me go.

Over the past nine years, me and Nick have had our issues with each other from us being together to now him being blocked from contacting me in any way. Funny that as I was scrolling TikTok the other day, he popped up. The last time I went to see him, was for his birthday in 2021 in Seattle, Washington. He tried to manipulate me into believing that if I loved him, I'd accept his infidelity, narcissistic beliefs and gaslighting tendencies. We got into a huge argument, and he kicked me out of his apartment at 1am. Let us not forget, this is a man "of the cloth" .. Do I still think about him? Absolutely. Do I wish we could've worked out? Damn right. Not only was he a man I thought I fell in love with, but he also was some of the best sex I've ever had. Looking back, I wasn't in love. It was just pure obsession. I do think he had potential to be an amazing man, however I respect and value myself so much more.

Nick, I know ultimately you'll read this because you can't stay away from me, but I hope you're well! Xo.

Dash

TAVON

Has anyone ever added you to their close friends randomly? Like, you don't know them, you just opened the app and saw the green circle? Well, that's exactly what happened with Tavon. I go viral a lot on social media which means an influx of followers and most times, it's too damn many to keep up with. It wasn't until I got on IG one day and checked my request folder that I saw hundreds of messages. As I scrolled through them, I stopped on one in particular, Tavon. I opened the message to see it was him reacting to my stories; roses here, heart eyes there for about 2 weeks. I went to his page and my goddamn!!! The man was FINE! Perfect chocolate skin, chiseled jaw, dripped in Louis Vuitton and certainly, a hood n*gga. Immediately, I double tapped his latest message then followed him. Next thing I know, GREEN CIRCLE! It wasn't anything there that he couldn't post on his regular ig story, but I was happy to be there! I started reacting to his story the same as he did mine and who would've thought the man would end up in my apartment, slutting me out and spitting in my mouth?

'I want to kiss and get fucked.' I posted to twitter. Twitter is the place where all my intrusive thoughts roam freely. I screenshot the post and posted it to my close friends on Instagram. At this point, I had already added Tavon to mine. The minute I posted, he responded.
"Let me kiss and fuck you."
I gasped reading his message because, excuse me? Now yes, I wanted to accept his offer but sometimes, you have to play a little hard to get. Plus, I had just moved into my new apartment and there was shit everywhere. I didn't even have a sofa! I had been drooling over this man since I saw him and if I could show you a picture, you'd be drooling too! Although I didn't want to lose my opportunity, it just wasn't the right time.
"I just moved in yesterday and if my place were more organized, I'd take you up on that." I replied.

First impressions are everything, so I was hoping he'd understand.
"I don't give a fuck about that. Send me your address" he responded.
"1 Lincoln Woods Way."

I wasted no time because if the n*gga didn't care that it looked like a tornado ravaged my apartment, neither did I! I jumped up, ran to the shower to freshen up and put on the shortest most 'I'm not trying to be sexy, but I look sexy as fuck' dress I could find.

Tavon arrived around 11:30pm and he looked even better in person. Shorter than I anticipated, he stood at 5'6. His layered Cuban link necklaces and Rolex watch, danced under the moonlight complimenting his chocolate skin. I thought to myself, 'You have to be this fresh to drop off some dick?' but I welcomed him in and closed the door. "Would you like something to drink?" I asked as he sat in one of the two arms chairs I had.
"Water if you have it." The strong Baltimore accent made my pussy throb.
I brought him a chilled bottle of water as we made conversation. "I'm not the one for small talk. We know what you're here for. Take your dick out." I said softly while biting my lip.
"Damn, I'm scared of you. You get straight to it, huh?" He joked.

I was hoping that his dick wasn't little, but I wasn't expecting him to pull out that big ass horse dick! I mean it was huge even on soft! The bigger my eyes got just looking at it, the bigger IT got. I immediately dropped to my knees. I started sucking it, stroking it, gently grazing it with my teeth then making it disappear in my throat.
"Ah fuck!" He moaned. "This what you had in store for me?"
I looked up at him and gave him a nonverbal 'yes' with my eyes. My juices now dripping down my

thighs, I needed him inside of me. He must've read my mind because after about 5 minutes of sucking his dick, he told me to lay on my back. As I sprawled out on the lush gray carpet, he kissed me long and hard followed by a trail of kisses down my stomach to my pussy. He didn't immediately devour me; he took his time teasing me. Soft bites on my inner thigh down to my toes then damn near put my whole foot in his mouth! He licked and kissed back up my calves and finally engulfed my fat ass pussy into his mouth. He didn't just eat my pussy, he made love to her. He sucked on my clit ever so gently then eased two fingers inside of me. I could tell he was a pro just by his rhythm. No matter how much I squirmed uncontrollably under him, he never stopped feasting. His tongue danced across my clit as if he was writing his ABC's. After cumming in his mouth, he continued to devour me. You know how fragile you get after a big orgasm? That was me. My body was so confused because I wanted him to keep going but I wasn't sure if I could handle it.

"Damn you taste good!" He said, as he kissed up my stomach. Once he reached my mouth, I grabbed his face and pulled him into me, kissing him long and hard. I felt his dick harden between my thighs and without warning, he thrusted into me, deep. He forced all 11 inches of that dick into me. My pussy

sucked him in like a vacuum. I let out a loud moan into his mouth as he took his time with me. Tavon slow stroked me to the beat of his own drum. The room was dark, but I could feel his eyes grazing over all over my body. His sweat dripped from his forehead onto my face, and I could no longer tell the difference between his sweat and my tears.

"Fuck me, just like that, please." I whimpered.
I didn't want him to stop. I needed him to force the orgasm out of me. Tavon then held his body up on his fist, sped up his stroke and slammed his hips into my pelvic destroying my pussy and as much as I wanted to talk my shit, I couldn't. I couldn't find the words. All I could muster up was 'YES'.
"You a pretty chocolate bitch." He growled. "Take that big dick you pretty bitch!"
Before I knew it, I was screaming and squirting all over his dick. "That's it. That's how I like it." He said.

As my body began to go limp, he pulled out and started feasting on me, again. He lapped up every bit of my juices like a kitten and didn't stop until he made me cum in his mouth. Tavon grabbed me by my ankles and flipped me over like a rag doll. I assumed the position, ass up face down. In my mind, I just knew my knees would be fucked up from carpet burns but baby, we'll just have to deal with that when we get to it! His thrust jolted me out of my thoughts.
"Ahhhhhh, fuck!" I screamed.
While Tavon thrusted into me, I threw my ass back on him. I could feel the carpet biting into my skin, but his moans were sending me over the edge, so I wasn't going to stop. His dick was vigorously massaging my walls and the pressure build up was none like I've ever experienced before!

"Yes Daddy! Fuck. Me. Just. Like. That!" I said through clenched teeth.

I thought I was going to explode. You know that feeling when they're so deep in your pussy, their strokes, the intensity, the pain, and pleasure coupled with their stamina and desire to please you? Yes. That. That feeling deep in your pussy where it just feels so good, you can't move, speak, or moan? Yes. That's exactly what I was experiencing.

"Give me that pussy like a good girl." His voice was deep. One hand now smushing my face into the floor with the other smacking my ass, he wasn't playing with me. He came prepared. My pussy was literally dripping, and I didn't want him to stop. He pounded me over and over and over again until I was screaming his name or at least I tried to.

"Tay...." I couldn't speak. Every time I went to open my mouth, nothing came out.

"Say it." He said, sharply. "What's my fucking name?!"

My words failed me.

"WHATS MY FUCKING NAME?!"

"DADDY!" I cried.

My body fell to the floor, and he collapsed on top of me. Tavon didn't stop fucking me though. He used his knee to push my leg up so now we're in the 'Magic Mountain' position - yes, google it ;).. I turned my upper body around just enough to reach and grab the back of his neck. He slowed his rhythm and at this point, I knew he was about to nut.

"Open your mouth" he said as he gripped the side of my face. He began to spit in my mouth. It wasn't a big glob of spit. It was very fine and silky and that told me one thing, his diet healthy as fuck! He leaned in to kiss me and the intimacy was driving me insane! Tavon rotated his hips in a circular motion grinding into me. His balls grazed across my clit with each circle which made me cum even harder than before! The grip he had on my face was getting tighter as I squeezed my pussy on his dick. I straightened my leg and arched my back. This position was the finisher. I reached both hands back to spread my ass open and in typical freaky n*gga fashion, he put his thumb in my butt. Now I don't like anything in my ass, but I didn't want to ruin the moment, so I went with it.

"Open that pussy up just like that, I want to feel you." He said, while giving me slow and aggressive yet gentle strokes. "Give me every drop of it" I moaned. "Every single fucking drop."

His dick now rock hard, deep in my tight, wet pussy, he leaned down, kissing my back then spit on it. The strokes got harder and harder.
"Fuck! I'm about to nut!"
He gripped the back of my neck.
"Give me that nut baby." I said to him.
I caught his rhythm, and we rocked the boat as my pussy swallowed up every inch and every drop of him. His body fell onto mine and we laid there. His dick was still throbbing and my pussy holding onto him. Now you may ask yourself, "Where was the condom?" Girl, there wasn't one. That man fucked the dog shit out of me, RAW and it was so good. And did I mention I was ovulating??? To answer your next question, no, I didn't get pregnant. Even though my period was 31, THIRTYFUCKINGONE days late, I wasn't pregnant. I was dickmatized for sure and for a while, I'd get upset when he was busy being the hood's favorite celebrity but oh baby, when he spun that block a couple weeks later, I put this pussy on

him really good because n*gga, when I call, YOU COME INSIDE .. pun intended.

Dash

SARAH

Did you think I was going to leave you hanging and not give you a story about my encounter with a woman??? Let me introduce you to Sarah.

I made a post on Instagram expressing how I needed a muse to be featured in my next promo video, preferably a woman. There were a lot of inquiries being that I was discounting the service, however, I advised that whoever I selected, had to come to me, was comfortable being on camera and comfortable with the fact that I wasn't blurring any identifying tattoos or scars, only their face. Sarah was one of the women that responded to the flyer via DM telling me that she would love to be massaged by me and that she had no problems with my stipulations. She asked if her husband could watch the service and

I agreed. Sarah sent me her payment and I sent her the location and all other details she would need for her appointment. For the next hour, I scrolled through her page just getting a glimpse of who she was and what she looked like. Although I don't discriminate, I did want a beautiful woman on my table. Sarah was more than that though. She had shoulder length honey blonde locs, caramel skin, and an essence about her that drew me in.

She was scheduled to come the next day, and I was more than prepared. Once they arrived, I went over my disclaimer, as I usually do and asked if they had any objections. I set up my camera, and ring light, and we got the show started. Her husband sat in a chair nearby, watching the entire thing. I stopped the massage every few minutes or so to make sure the camera was still recording and to adjust the angle. While I stretched her legs out, I noticed her pussy was dripping fucking wet. Immediately, it turned me on. Of course, I didn't say anything, I kept my thoughts to myself. Once I flipped her over and set her up into me to massage her back, I was shocked by how tight she embraced me. I could tell that she needed this. I finished out Sarah's massage and when I went to stop the camera, IT HAD DIED!!! I was pissed.

"You're not going to believe this, but my camera died." I said with irritation. "I don't know how much of it was saved. I'll charge it and see what I have. Thank you so much for coming, I hope you both enjoy your evening!"

They gathered their things and left. I was pissed. There was no room for small talk. Although I wasn't rude to them, all I wanted to do was shower, charge the camera and review the footage, if there was any.

After my shower, I was surprised to see that she had sent me a dm not long after they left.
"I can come back tonight if you didn't get the content you needed." The message read.
I would love for her to come back! The way her body responded to me earlier, gave me chills. Her moans were so soft. My fingers melted into her skin. The way she shivered with every single touch assured me that she was present, mentally. Not to mention, her pussy was soaked, leaving a huge wet spot on my sheets.
"I would love that!" I responded to her.
I didn't mind going through a full massage again – for the content, of course. We arranged a time and I waited. When I finally checked my camera, I saw that it had recorded the entire session. There was no need to do it again but, it was too late. I wasn't going to cancel her. I can read energy and body language very well and if I knew like I knew, Sarah wanted me just as much as I wanted her.
"I'm outside." She texted.
I didn't respond, I just went to let her in.

"Welcome back." I smiled.

I went over my disclaimer and consent again because at this point, it's imbedded in my brain. I know the line may be slightly blurred now, but I still take my business serious. We'll get to play later. I undressed her and she climbed up on my table. I turned the music on and got to massaging. This time, her husband wasn't there, and I could feel that she was a bit more comfortable. Her being relaxed allowed me to pour into her in ways that I didn't earlier. When I flipped her over and sat her on my lap to massage her breasts, our eyes met. She let out a long, deep sigh as I cupped her titty and grazed it across my bottom lip, breathing on it. Sarah threw her head back placing one hand on my thigh and the other around the back of my neck. I traced her nipple with my lips over and over again.

"Please." She whispered.

"Can I put my mouth on you?" I asked softly.

"Yes. Please."

I stuck out my tongue, flicking it back and forth across her nipple before putting in my mouth and gently sucking it. Sarah grinded herself into me. I switched over to the other nipple and gave it the same care and attention. Her nipples were like super large pink gumdrops. I felt them grow in my mouth and it was at this moment I knew I would fuck her senseless. Maybe not today, but someday. Someday soon.

I continued teasing her as I laid her back onto the table. It was time for her yoni massage. I began with my thumb and slow circular motions around her clit. Her breathing was heavy. I knew that if she didn't control her breathing, she wouldn't enjoy her massage like I needed her to.

"Take a deep breath and control your breathing." I spoke.

My voice was low, calm, and steady. We both can't be excited. She did as I told her and steadied her breathing. I massaged her to the rhythm of the music, taking her on a journey but never too fast. I wanted this to build up. I wanted her to explode in ways she never has. While massaging her pussy, I slid my body off the table so that now, I'm laying between her legs. My face was inches away from her love garden. I began to kiss her inner thighs, never missing a beat. Sarah never stopped moaning and never stopped adhering to her quick lesson in breath work.

"Is this okay?" I asked between every kiss. I wanted her consent with everything that I did to her. After all, we were recording. "Yes." Her moans were so damn sweet!

I stopped massaging and kiss her pussy.

"Is this okay?" I questioned.

"Yes."

I licked her pussy.

"Do you want this?"

"Yes." Her breathing getting heavier.

"Tell me."

I wanted to hear the words out of her mouth that she wanted it.

"I want it. Please." Sarah begged.

"What do you want?" I questioned in between kisses and licks. "Please eat my pussy. Please."

I didn't ask any more questions. I dove right into her sea headfirst. I couldn't tell the difference between my saliva and her ocean. It had been a while since I'd eaten pussy and I was starving. I ate her pussy like my life depended on it. When she came in my mouth, I kept eating. This was for her pleasure, absolutely, but mine also. She moaned out my name, begging me for more and I gave her exactly that. Her hands glided through my short blonde hair. I slid my hands under her, gripping her waist. Sarah grinded her pussy in my face and I knew she was about to cum again. I slurped her clit into my mouth and swirled my tongue as fast as I could, encouraging her to let it all out. She did.

I got up and disappeared to the back of my apartment. I re- emerged with a bag of dicks. Dicks of all shapes, sizes, and colors. I pulled out a slim, black dildo, that curved specifically for g-spot stimulation. Did I mention it had 8 vibrating patterns? "Is this okay?" I asked as Sarah laid stretched out on the table, playing with her pussy.

"Yes." She replied softly.
I covered the dildo with a condom and repositioned myself between her thighs. No, I didn't strap up, I wanted to start slow with her. I feasted on her once more but this time, with the black dick stoking the inside of her, vibrating on the heartbeat setting. Ladies, you know what I'm talking about. She could no longer contain herself or her breathing. I picked up my pace fucking her with the dildo, my tongue never leaving her clit. Sarah bounced and grinded on the table, catching my rhythm.
"Fuucckkkkk!!! I'm cumming!!!!" she moaned.
"Yes you are." I said. "That pussy is cumming so hard."

Sarah laid there panting, out of breath, freshly eaten and fucked.

"Sit on my face." I said to her.

She peeled herself off the table, giving room for me to lay back. She mounted my face, looked me in my eyes and caressed my cheeks. I locked my arms around her thighs and never let her look away. I devoured that lady so damn good. I stroked her back softly with my fingertips before smacking ass. I wanted her to cum in my mouth one last time before I sent her on her back to her husband. I stuck out my tongue and allowed her to slide that pussy up and down it, leaving a trail of her juices.

Sarah sat back on my chest, legs trembling. I reached up to give her some soft touches to slowly bring her body down from the heights it had just experienced.
"I've never been with a woman before and that... That was mind-blowing." She said.
I just smiled at her because in my mind and experience, being a woman's first, was a world of fucking trouble. After Sarah dismounted me, I gave her a towel and cloth to freshen up. I went into the other bathroom to do the same.

After that encounter, she would text me often, come over get her nut off and go back home to play wifey. She expressed how she wanted a divorce, didn't want me to move out of state, wanted to take care of me, a bunch of shit. For me, it was just fun, I didn't want anything serious. It was all fun and games until a year or two ago, her husband sent me a message telling me that he KNEW it was her in a video we made of me eating her pussy. One particular scene in the video, while eating her pussy, I looked into the camera and winked. If you follow me on twitter, you know exactly what video I'm speaking of. He told me he felt I was winking at him in a "Ha ha, I got your bitch" kind of way. He asked me how long I've been seeing her, told me how embarrassed he was, that they're getting divorced, you know, the whole thing. Baby that had nothing to do with me and after she got pissed because I didn't give her what she want when she wanted it, I had to remove myself from the situation entirely.

Her name popped up in my orders recently and I took that opportunity to reach out to her.
"Let me eat your pussy." I texted.
"How you cut me off and expect me to come running when you want me back."
I didn't even respond. I wanted her on my face again, absolutely, but I didn't want it if it came with all the extra shit. Her question was valid but lady, can I eat your pussy again or NOT?????

Dash

VANCE

"I want to feel you deep inside of me." I
managed to say while slurping on Vance's dick as if it
was a sour green apple lollipop. I made sure not to
lose eye contact. I searched his eyes and waited on his
body language to ask the magic words.
"Are you bleeding or are you bleeding bleeding?" He
asked.
I ignored him for a while. I wanted to make love to
his dick with my mouth, first. I loved sucking dick. It
was one of my best skills. I always made them lose

their mind and just seeing them so helpless from my mouth alone, made my pussy soaking wet. I deep throated his dick and held it there for about 5 seconds.

"Ahhh FUCK!!!" He moaned. "Do that shit again!" Me being the obedient angel that I am, I obliged. He exhaled loudly then grabbed my face to pull me up to him. Vance kisses were magical. He palmed the back of my head just right with his thumb tucked under my ear. His lips fit perfectly between mine. Our tongues glided across one another creating their own little dance.

"I'm barely bleeding." I whispered. "Fuck me please." At this point, I didn't want him inside of me, I needed him inside me. My pussy was pulsating like crazy and the only way it was going to stop, was for Vance to put me out of my misery. "Ok."
That was it. That was the magic word. I jumped up and walked swiftly to the linen closest. I grabbed three large towels and placed them around the chocolate brown ottoman that sat in the center of my living room. I watched him as he slipped off his navy-blue work pants, then his compression shorts. Before he dropped his pants to the ground, he pulled out a condom. It was a black wrapper, so I automatically knew it was my favorite brand, SKYN!

I dropped down to my knees and crawled over to where he was standing. While he reached to take his shirt off, I reached for his dick to put back into my warm mouth. I started sucking, stroking his dick with both hands. Unable to keep his balance, he pulled out and told me to bend over. I turned around and bent over the ottoman, laying my face into the rich leather. I made sure to keep my arch perfect and steady. I felt him kneel behind me and spread my legs with his knees. I waited in anticipation. Vance ripped the condom wrapper with his teeth and rolled the condom down his shaft. He put his hand on my lower back and the other on my hip. It didn't take long before... Hold up, pause. Let me introduce you to Vance... Mmm, Vance.

I met Vance through social media. One of my old coworkers made a status asking fathers of young girls, if they liked women calling them 'Daddy' during sex. I thought it was an interesting conversation, so I followed the replies. Vance was one of the commenters. I commented under him saying "That's a fine ass dad up there" referring to Vance and before I knew it, he had sent me a friend request. That practically was an invitation into his inbox, and I did exactly that!
"I'm just coming here to say that God took his time with you! That's all, bye for now." I typed.
I didn't expect a response back as fast as I had received one, but I was pressed see what he said.
"Wait, don't go yet, come back."

I was a little excited. I flirted with him for a while, almost every day. I began to send him tasteful nudes of myself as a way to entice him. He countered my nudes with his own, sending me dick pics and I started to question myself on how much longer I could wait. My patience was growing thin. His dick was perfect! Nice, chocolate, thick. I was in love with a picture. Was I crazy? Probably, but oh well. I finally worked up the nerve and invited him over to my apartment after 3 days. Now I know you're reading this questioning THREE days? Girl, yes. Be thankful I didn't say one. We planned for him to come over the following week.

Here it was, the day I would finally see Vance in person. I was like a kid in a candy store. One of my friends cancelled our friends date earlier that morning so I just sat there, waiting. It was a hot summer day and I sat on my couch in a sports bra and booty shorts.
"I'm outside."
When I read his text, my palms started sweating. Why was I nervous? This for sure wasn't my first rodeo.
"Come upstairs. Apartment F. The door is open." I responded.
I sat on the couch waiting for him to come inside. I heard him marching up the stairs to my apartment. I tried to hide my excitement but was unsuccessful. As he opened the door, I felt like I was in school all over again, having a crush on a classmate. He plopped down on the couch next to me and I threw my legs over his.
"How was work?" I asked.
"Work was cool. My relief was late that's why I'm late getting to you."

Vance had messaged me earlier in the day to tell me he'd be late for this exact reason. He was a bus driver, and I knew how unpredictable his schedule could be. After about 5 minutes, I got tired of the small talk. I wanted him in the worst way. I stood up, locked the door then pulled him out of his seat. He stood hovering over me, all 6'6 of him. He looked so damn good. He had shoulder length locs with a few grey strands and a low-cut salt and pepper beard. His eyes were almond shaped and dark brown in color. His voice was deep yet soft and sexy. He wrapped one hand around my waist and the other palmed my freshly cut bald head. He tilted his head to the side and kissed my soul. His lips were fucking perfect! Soft and succulent. He pulled me into him as his fingertips sunk into my cocoa butter skin. I didn't want him to let me go.

"Take these off" I said as I fumbled with the buckle on his belt. He did exactly that. I pushed him down onto the couch because I wanted him in my mouth. My warm, wet mouth was watering for his dick. His dick sprung up out of his pants, precum already dripping from the head. I smiled to myself because I knew that I was the cause of it. I kissed all 11 inches of his dick. I licked up and down his shaft, teasing him. Maintaining eye contact, I went down on him. I came up and went down again. Over and over. He threw his head back and let out a long sigh.

"I want to be the one to relieve your stress every day after work." I said softly, and I meant every word of it.

The way he was responding to me let me know that he was enjoying himself. His moans got louder the faster I moved. I reached up grabbing his phone because I wanted him to record me. I don't know what it is with me and cameras, but I love being recorded. He propped his phone up on the pillow, angled it directly at me and used his hands to grab both sides of my face. I stared directly into the lens of the camera as he moved his hips to work himself in and out of my mouth. There was spit everywhere! My makeup was smeared but I didn't care. I shoved his

dick in my mouth and down my throat, taking in every single inch. No gagging. I held it there for about 5 seconds. I had to make sure he had footage to watch later. "Ahhh, FUCK! Do that shit again!" He moaned.
A sly smile crept across my face as I did it again and again until he could no longer control himself.

Shall we now pick up where we left off earlier?
It didn't take long before he was inside of me. He stroked me so damn slow. Slow and steady. I wanted to feel him and he me. He was driving me insane. I was falling in love with this dick by the second. It's almost as if he'd already knew my body the way he handled me. He was so gentle and attentive. The touch of his hands all over my body, then gripping my ass while trying to hold back his nut sent chills down my spine. Vance interrupted my thoughts as his strokes became faster and harder. Each thrust was more powerful than the last. He didn't say a word. Absolutely nothing. I felt the beads of sweat drip from him onto me. The smell of sweet, hot, sweaty not to mention bloody sex, filled the air. He pulled me into him, squeezing me. I knew he was almost at his peak, so I took advantage of it. I started grinding my ass on him.
"That's right, give me that dick." I whispered.
I was going to talk shit now because the ball was in my court. I knew he couldn't hold out any longer especially not with my juicy ass bouncing on him.
"Give me that nut." My voice was soft and seductive.

I was ready for it. Wherever he decided to put it, I was ready. I propped one leg up to give him more

access to me. "FUUUCCKKK!" He cried out.
"You like that?" I questioned. "Tell me you like this pussy."

"I like it." His voice almost a whisper.
What a beautiful ride. His strokes became harder.
"You're gonna make me nut, Dash!"
I could almost hear his heart beating out of his chest.
"Give it to me then."
As I finished my sentence, I felt Vance's body tense up, so I started to throw ass and grip his dick to make sure I got every single drop out of him.
"Damn that was good." He said, his breath trying to catch up to him. I winked at him, stood up and walked to the bathroom. I immediately started the shower to wash Aunt Flo's wrath off me. I climbed in and to my surprise, Vance pulled back the shower curtain and joined me.

Climbing out of the shower, Vance wrapped a towel around his waist and sat on the edge of my bed. I came and sat between his legs and started massaging his feet. Dick so good it had me massaging HIS feet!! We had a long conversation about life and how we are raised. I got so lost in him that I lost track of time. "I have to pick up my son from school. I wish I could stay here in this moment with you all day." I said. "Yeah, same here. I thoroughly enjoyed you." We both got dressed and left.

On our way out the door, we hugged and kissed as if we were a couple sending each other off for the day. He carried me on his back, down the stairs and out to my car. Still to this day, Vance has given me some of the best dick of my life. Not to be confused with the best sex from Nick. I used to joke with my friends saying I was dickmatized but baby I was not playing. He had me whipped. Any man that will run a red light with no care in the world, is a man after my own heart. We kept in contact up until recently, I hired him to be my trainer, but we had a falling- out to the point he blamed me for him and his girlfriend breaking up. Anyway, I still watch the video we made and if you're on my Onlyfans page, you've seen it. Maybe one day, I'll tell the story of how my sister walked in while I was riding his dick on my mother's couch, completely naked with thigh high boots on. Green thigh high boots that he picked out.

Dash

HECTOR

This story is wild as hell and I'm cackling just typing it. I fucked my landlord y'all. I was 20 years old and lived with my mom at the time so technically, he was her landlord. I wasn't paying any bills and whatever I wanted to do, I did. No, it wasn't acceptable in her home but hey, a rebel will be a rebel, right? Hector was a sweet little man, pun intended, and he didn't live too far from us. He'd come over about once a week or so because there was always something for him to fix. Sometimes, he'd stop by on his way home just to say hi to us.

Hector had a thing for me, and everyone could see it. I didn't mind flirting back with him or even flirting in the presence of my mother because to her, it was innocent. Boy oh boy, was she wrong!

She'd be at work the majority of the time he came to fix something, and I was always home, so I'd wait for him to get there to let him in and explain whatever the problem was. One time in particular, Hector asked me if he could give me a gift. We were standing on the back patio, and I assured him that him gifting me whatever, was okay with me. He pulled out a wad of cash and peeled back a crisp $100 bill and handed it to me.

"Oh my gosh! Hector, thank you so much!" I exclaimed.

I wasn't expecting him to give me money, hell, I didn't have any expectations on his 'gift', but I damn sure wasn't going to turn it down.

"You're welcome Cookie." He responded, in his thick Mexican accent. "I just wanted to do something nice for you."

My nickname is Cookie so don't get lost as you're reading. I gave him a hug and he left.

A couple weeks had passed since I saw him, and I wondered where he had been. You can't just give me money and disappear, or can he? Hector was the landlord so he couldn't stay too far away for too long. I occupied myself until I saw him again.

The bathroom sink kept getting clogged up and wouldn't drain the way it was supposed to, so my mother told me that Hector would be coming over today to fix it and I tried to conceal my excitement. Honestly, I was a bit depressed with where my life was so seeing Hector, made me excited. It was sometimes, the highlight of my day.

I was chilling in my room, watching my favorite show, Judge Judy, when I heard a knock at the door. We didn't get many visitors, so I knew who it was. I jumped up and went to let him in.

"Hey Cookie, how are you?" He asked.

"I'm good Hector, how are you?"

We exchanged pleasantries and hugs.

"What seems to be the problem with the sink?" Hector questioned as he led the way upstairs.

"I don't know it may be clogged with hair, which we know isn't mine."

We both laughed. I watched him as he worked, running back and forth to his truck for his supplies. Eventually, I went back to my room to watch tv as he worked.

"Alright Cookie, I think I fixed the problem." He said.

My bedroom was right next to the bathroom so I could hear everything he did and said. I walked out to the hallway to see him packing up.

"I'm taking these things out to the truck, and I'll be right back to check the sink one last time."

"Okay." I responded.

I stood in the hallway, waiting for him to come back. Hector made sure the sink was squared away before approaching me. "Cookie, you're so beautiful, you know that?"

"That you Hector." I said smiling at him.

He got closer and closer then grabbed my waist and came in for a kiss. His fucking breath smelled like sour milk, and it instantly made my stomach turn. I had never been with a man that wasn't black, so I wasn't sure if this is what Mexican men usually smelled like or what but baby, it was stinking so bad. (I later learned that it was just him.) I pulled back after the first kiss and giggled nervously. He grabbed my hand and pulled my into my bedroom, closing the door behind him.

"I want to taste you. I've been wanting to taste you since you moved in." He said.

Hector was kissing on my neck now and it was hard for me to decipher if I was turned on or off. I knew I'd have to sit in a bath and scrub this sour smell off of me.

"Can I taste you?" he asked, interrupting my thoughts.

"Sure."

I didn't know how to say no. I was hoping that he'd sense my ball of nerves and take that as a no but, he didn't. He began pulling my pajama pants down.

"Lay on the bed." He spoke.

I did as I was told but I covered my face not only to block his breath but because I was nervous as hell. Is somebody going to come home? Is he taking advantage of me because he gave me money? So many questions raced through my brain.

I was quickly jolted out of my thoughts the moment he started eating my pussy. It felt so good. The way he maneuvered his tongue up and down my pussy, flickering it across my clit, sucking on it and my lips. I forgot about the horrid smell and started to work myself into his mouth. He looked up at me with a mouth full of pussy. He started to speak.

"Uh uh, put it back in your mouth." I said.

I tightly gripped a handful of his hair with one hand, massaging my nipples with the other. His mouth never left my pussycat again. He never came up for air, never spoke another word and I was thankful for that.

I had never had my pussy eaten like this before. Now, I've gotten head, yes, but it was only for a couple minutes to get it wet enough to fuck. Keep in mind that I was 20 years old and what I thought I knew about sex, didn't come close to the world of interesting and exciting things that were out there. Hector ate my pussy for about 10 minutes before I came in his mouth. He came up with a big ass smile on his face and cum dripping from his beard. "You taste so good Cookie." He said, reaching for his belt buckle. Now this ain't that type of party, I didn't sign up for this. Hector wanted to fuck and well; I was shocked by the head he had on his shoulders so maybe I'll be surprised but what he had down under. Or so I thought. That man pulled out that itty bitty shrimp and I just about lost it. My clit was bigger than that thing! "Dash, it'll get bigger." I thought to myself. "It's just...soft." Dear reader, I regret to inform you that it indeed, did not get bigger. Hector went in for the kill and this is when I knew I was a good actor. You would've thought he was nailing me to the cross the way I performed.

"Yes, fuck me like that!" I 'moaned'. Deep down on the inside, my blood was boiling. Sir, take your clitoris and GET OUT of my house!!! I was a people pleaser even down to sex. I didn't want to hurt his feelings, me and my family had to live here. Crazy how all of this was flooding my mind and I was stilling screaming out oh's and ah's.

Hector nutted and caught it in his hand, and I didn't even notice he was done. I smiled at him and walked to the bathroom to clean myself up.
"I'm heading out Cookie. I left you a nice gift on your dresser. I'll lock up for you." He yelled out to me.
Shit, that was the least he could do. I knew it was money because he hadn't come with anything else. I took a quick shower and now that I had a couple dollars, I was going outside.

About 30 minutes later, my mother walked in the door from work.

"Hey Cook. Did Hector come to fix the sink?" she asked.
"Yup. He sure did! It was hair trapped down in the drain. He said if you need anything else, to let him know."
I continued getting dressed, grabbed my $200 'gift' and headed out the door. I saw Hector a few more times after that day but nothing intimate happened. Maybe he knew I was faking. Either way, he continued to come over to fix up the property. I'd stay in my room for most of the time he was there or if I knew he was coming, I'd be outside somewhere. He had a key; he could let himself in. I wanted to avoid him as much as possible because I didn't want him getting any ideas. I remained cordial but that breath was always hot. Now that I knew how it smelled up close, I felt like I could smell it across the room.

Once I moved out of mothers house, I never seen Hector again. It wasn't until I picked my son up from daycare one day that I noticed Hector's house sat directly across from the damn school. I began seeing him every single day, morning, and afternoon. I'd speak to him, but I always kept it moving. No conversation whatsoever. Hector is on my Facebook page and may like a photo every now and again to make his presence known.

And no, our rent was never discounted because I'm sure that was a question on your mind! Lmao!!

Dash

TERRANCE

You ever wanted someone so badly and when you finally got them, you just weren't impressed? Like, what the fuck was all the hype about? That's exactly what happened with Terrance. It pissed me off and it isn't that he's a terrible lay, sex with him just isn't what I thought it would be. Let's take a short stroll down memory lane.

I met Terrance in 2020 on my first massage tour. His girlfriend had booked a couples massage with me and although I had communicated with him through social media, I didn't know I'd be massaging him until she sent me a photo of the pair. When I saw the photo of him, I instantly felt some type of way because I previously had an awful encounter with him and the co-host of his podcast. I was supposed to be a guest on the show and after I drove 4 hours to their studio, neither of them were answering my calls or texts. I didn't want to massage him, but I began to feel like I had a point to prove. I wanted to confront him in person, so I agreed to massage them and impatiently waited for the day that he'd be on my table.

April was finally here, and I'd get to meet him in person to potentially speak my peace, no spellcheck. When they entered the room, Tasha, his girlfriend, came in first.
"Hi guys! Welcome in. How are you?" I exclaimed.
"Good." They responded simultaneously.
"I'm Dash, it's nice to meet you both!"
"Should I tell her who I am?" Terrance asked Tasha.
"I know exactly who you are." I shot back. "Do you want to have this conversation now or later?" I responded with a smug look on my face.

"Later." he said.
I gave a fake smile because of course you don't want to address the issue right now but also; this wasn't the time or the place to do so.
"Again, my name is Dash and I'll be your sensual masseuse for the evening. With your sensual massage, I'll be massaging every inch of your body very sensually, very erotically, very slowly and very seductively. Your yoni and lingam massages are included in your sensual massages however if you choose not to get it, that's completely fine with me, it will not take away from your sensual experience. If you do decide to get it, I will use non-latex gloves to

do so. In no way will I penetrate you, put my mouth on you or try to have sex with you. I'm very thorough with consent so when I get to your pleasure zones, I'll ask you is it okay if I massage this area. I need you to verbally say yes or no. At any point if you get uncomfortable, please immediately let me know. I'll be sure to stop whatever it is I'm doing to accommodate you and make you more comfortable. Allow yourself to be present in this space. You're allowed to touch me, talk to me, moan, groan, scream, however your body chooses to release, I welcome it. Shall we begin?"

Tasha got on my table first. She was fucking gorgeous. The epitome of a New York woman. I wanted to show off just how great I am at catering to the woman's body but as much attention as I gave her body, she gave me nothing. I mean absolutely nothing. Not a moan, not a groan, not a shiver down her spine, nothing! I say to my clients all the time that their massage is only going to be as great as they allow it to be hence the 'Allow yourself to be present in this space' speech. Maybe she was present and just had a different way of showing it. I was confident in my work so I knew I had done everything I could to make her experience a good one. As Terrance sat idly by, I whispered in her ear, "Your massage is complete. Take your time getting up." I exited the room to quickly wash my hands and face. I returned to clean up my table and dress it in preparation for Terrance.

"Are you ready?" I asked, pointing to Terrance.
He jumped up and quickly undressed. Once on my

table, I selected a different playlist and got to work introducing his body to my touch.

"Take three deep breaths for me." I said softly in his ear.

I traced his spine applying minimal pressure following his breaths.

"Just relax and focus on your breathing for me."

I closed my eyes and let the soft, raspy voice of Lalah Hathaway, serenade me as I got into my groove. I moved from his back to his butt, down his legs and to his feet. This is the part of the massage where I relax your entire body because once I flip you over, the fun begins.

"Flip over for me." I whispered to him.

Terrance rolled his body over and I began with his shoulders. I glided my hands down his chest sweeping my DD's across his face. He inhaled deeply as the sweet smell of my perfume, Essence by Pure Intimacy, filled his nostrils. I massaged his stomach never lifting my breasts from his face. I could feel Terrance's body giving into me. I climbed onto the table and straddled him, reverse cowgirl style to massage his legs. He started gripping my ass and I felt his dick growing under me. That's exactly what I was waiting on. I lifted my head to see Tasha watching intently. I honestly forgot she was there. In one swift motion, still on his lap, I turned to face him. I sat him up into me to massage his back, neck, and shoulders once again. As I laid him down, I allowed the oil to do its job as I slid off him and in between his legs.

It was now the time for his lingam massage. I wanted to make it interactive for Tasha, so I invited her over and instructed her to massage his chest while

I massaged his dick. I used one hand to stroke him as the other guided her on what to do.

'Put your nipple in his mouth.' I mouthed to her. She did exactly that. I watched as he groped her. In my mind, I was wishing it was me. Terrance was fine as hell! He was brown skin with the most perfect facial features. Structured jaw, gorgeous brown eyes, soft lips.. or at least I imagined they were. I was impressed with the way he handled her but even more impressed with the size of his dick. Y'all know I have a thing for big dicks! The more I stroked it, the bigger it got, and I do mean BIG! It was long, thick, vein-ny, heavy, juicy, you know, all the things us women love! I wanted nothing more than to sit on it. Tasha's movements interrupted my thoughts as Terrance had instructed her to sit on his face. She climbed up on the table and now me and her were face to face. This is my type of party because a spontaneous threesome? Yes, please. I was too wrapped up in my professionalism though, that I didn't allow it to go there. Apparently, it wasn't just me who Tasha didn't respond to because even with Terrance beneath her, devouring her pussy, she didn't make a sound.

I took my focus off them and went deeper into my imagination. I imagined just him and I in the room, knocking lamps off the dresser, chairs falling over. You know that crazy, rough yet passionate intimacy you really only ever see in movies? I continued massaging his dick to my visions until he exploded in my hands. I eased myself off the table to the restroom once more to clean myself up and it was in that moment I realized just how turned on I was. My pussy was soaking wet! I went back out to the room and Terrance was already dressed. I thanked them for booking me and they left.

For some time, I flirted with Terrance on Instagram to the point he wanted me to be him and Tasha's anniversary gift and to answer your question, no, it didn't happen. I wasn't upset that it didn't happen. I knew that in time, I would have them...or him but now that you have the backstory, let's hop to 2023. On one of his episodes, he mentioned how he doesn't want head anymore, he wants throat and neck. Interestingly enough, I had exactly what he was looking for, so I sent him a DM.
"Pencil me your schedule next Wednesday, please."
"For what?" He responded.
"Out of all the times I've told you I wanted to eat you up, my schedule finally permits so, pencil me in your schedule for Wednesday, thank you."
"I'd like that. We'll be recording around 9:30PM so you can come any time after that."
"That works for me. I'll see you Wednesday at 10."
Plan set. Now we wait.

Sunday was here and as I began packing and preparing for my trip to Baltimore, I decided to do a quick cleanse with Benefiber. Usually, the bloating will be gone within 24 hours so three scoops it is! Lord knows I'd regret that decision later. I got my things together and was on the road by midnight. I arrived in Baltimore at 7AM, just in time for me to clean myself up and get ready for my clients. Time seemed to fly by and before I knew it, it was Wednesday. The anticipation was building but I wasn't quite sure if Terrance had taken me serious or not. It had been three years of back and forth flirting with me saying I was coming to see him. He was probably just writing it off as me playing games again. I pulled out my phone and texted him.

"Hiiiii Terranceeeeeee! I was serious about coming to see you today. If you'd still like to see me, I need your address."

About 10 minutes later, Terrance responded with his address. Now the butterflies started to sink in or was it the Benefiber? Here I am thinking I'd be cleaned out by now but no, my stomach was in knots! I went to the gym and drunk a gallon of water hoping for some movement through my intestines, but nothing came from it. I was too scared to eat thinking that if I did, it wouldn't pass soon enough and that I'd be on the road, shitty as hell. I sat in a squat position for 8 minutes thinking this would be it, but a fool is what I was. I got up and went straight to the shower because time was ticking. If I was going to get to his house on time, I needed to stop fucking around and get myself together. I'd rather my stomach hurt than have hemorrhoids from straining.

Dressed and smelling delicious, I headed out the door. I set my GPS and got straight on the road. Terrance texted me when I was about 30 minutes away to see if I was still coming so I responded with a photo of my GPS. I pulled up to his house and as I got out the car, his assistant was locking his door. I started to get back in the car because I didn't want her seeing me, but I walked up to the door instead.
"Hi! How are you?" I asked

"Hey Dash! How are you?"
I'm sure she remembered me from when they finally got it right and had me on an episode but still, it's 10:30 at night and I'm pulling up to your boss' house? I didn't want her in my nor his business.
Terrance opened the door interrupting our short conversation, but I was happy that he did!
"Hey you." I spoke
"Hey, what's going on?"
Now, wait a damn minute. That's all I get? Here I am driving 4 hours AGAIN and all I get is a "Hey, what's going on?" N*gga you better put some excitement in your voice! Pick me up off the ground or something, goddamn!
I walked up the stairs to his place with him following closely behind me. Once in, he finally gave me a hug.
"You look great!" He exclaimed.
"Thank you! I've been in the gym, you know, unbigging my back." I giggled.
"Your back looks great!"
I wasn't sure if he was talking about my actual back or my ass because he asked me to do a 360.
Either way, both my ass and back looked good.
"I'm just waking up plus me and my assistant just got into an argument, so I apologize about my grogginess." He said.
"It's okay, I understand."
I mean yes, I did understand but sir, I didn't come here for that. I came here to eat that dick up and go about my business.

While Terrance cooked himself something to eat, I thumbed through his mini library, peaking at his interest. We made small talk for a while and when he was done, he sat next to me on the sofa. He wrapped his arm around me and stroked my arm with his fingertips. The way Terrance looked at me was very different from the way he's looked at me before. I couldn't quite put my finger on it, but I felt like he was trying to see my soul through my eyes.

"I didn't realize how beautiful you were Dash, and I don't mean physically. I've been watching you on Instagram and just seeing your personal growth and your maturity is very attractive."

"I'm flattered." I replied softly. "Thank you."

It felt nice to have someone notice my efforts and the work I've been doing on myself.

"Before this evening goes anywhere, I want to discuss boundaries." I said.

"You know we don't have to rush into anything, right?" Terrance asked.

"Of course, but I feel like boundaries are an important conversation to have. I don't want us to be knee deep into anything and I have to stop you because you're doing something I don't like or I'm doing something you don't like."

"Okay. You're right, lay it on me."

Terrance sat up on the couch, eager to hear me out.

"I don't like anything anal. Not your thumb. Not your tongue and especially not your dick." I said.

"Understood."

"I want to be your slut. Don't show me any mercy. Talk filthy to me, I mean disgustingly filthy. Call me out my name. I respond to bitch very well." I smiled. "Choke me. Spit on me. Nut on my face and rub it in... Shall I continue?"

I stopped speaking because he looked terrified! I giggled on the inside because he talk all this kinky shit on social media and his podcast, but my little list of kinks is what has him stunned?

"I...."
I stared at him intently through my glasses.
"I just didn't know we were going the distance tonight."
"That wasn't the plan but if we do, I want you to know what will turn me on." I replied.
"Do you like being told what to do?" He asked.
"Yes."
"Stand up and take your dress off."
The tone of his voice had changed to be more softer yet stern.
I did as I was told. I was completely naked under my tight- fitting, maxi dress. It showed every curve, and I was very intentional with wearing it. I sat back down on the couch.
"Can you take these off?" I questioned, pointing to his shorts.
"I can." He responded.

He raised his hips off the couch and pulled his shorts off. I stood up preparing to kneel in front of him but looked around the room for a pillow. It's almost as if he read my mind because he raced to get one out of a nearby closet. He placed the pillow on the floor in front of him and I knelt down. Kissing his dick all over, I watched it go from gummy to rock hard, pun intended, Iykyk. My, my, my. I waited three years for this moment, and it was finally here. I took him into my mouth, starting with the head, first. Inch by inch, I ate him up, just as I promised. Him wanting throat just kept replaying in my mind. I would massage his dick with my lips and tongue then with my hands and finally engulfing his dick and holding it in my throat.

"Goddamn!" He moaned. "Look at me while you have all that dick in your mouth!"

I looked up at him as best as I could with my eyes peeking over my glasses. I continued to stroke his dick with one hand while the other played with his balls and my mouth on the tip. We stayed here for about 10 minutes. Now with my track record, my mouth has made men cum in far less time, but I wanted this to last. I've waited too long to just suck a lil' dick and go about my business.

"I want to feel this dick in my pussy." I said, while smacking his dick on my face.

"Get up and go get on the bed."

I jumped up and practically ran to the bed with Terrance a step behind me. I sprawled out on his bed and began to play with my pussycat. He pulled me to the edge and started feasting in my love garden. With one hand, he massaged my pussy lips while the other penetrated me. Meanwhile, his tongue danced on my clit but not in an overstimulating kind of way. The pressure that was building up had me ready to explode.

Terrance lapped up every bit of my juices then came up to kiss me. His lips were perfect just had I imagined the day he was on my table. After slipping on a condom, his dick took a deep dive into my pussy making me gasp for air. It filled me up just like I knew it would. He took his time with me while staring into my eyes. You know the dick that's so good you almost slip up and say, 'I love you'? Well as many times as I've said it in these chapters, I've probably wanted to damn near tell everybody I loved them! Terrance slow stroked me, in and out. In and out. He never took his eyes off of me. In my head, I was still trying to find the words for the way he looked at me. He watched me intently. Did he think I was going to steal or was he waiting for this moment just as I had been for the last three years and couldn't believe it was happening? Either way, here we were.

"You like that?" He questioned.

His voice almost a whisper. Initially, I didn't hear what he said, and I knew if I said 'huh', it may ruin the mood so instead I just moaned "Yes", you can never go wrong with that.

The dick was good, but something was missing. It was lacking enthusiasm, chemistry, intimacy. My pussy was wet but baby, it gets wetter!!! I just went with the motions. It wasn't that I wasn't enjoying myself because I was, hell, I was about to tell him I loved him. I just thought it would be better than it was. Terrance interrupted my thoughts by telling me to go back to the living room and to bend over the ottoman. The ottoman was placed in front of a mirror and who doesn't love watching themselves get smashed to smithereens? It's something about the eye contact through the mirror, me watching you, you watching me, that just blows my mind. Maybe this would be the moment that the intimacy and chemistry would be heightened.

Terrance disappeared to the back of his apartment and reappeared with some oil.

"I know it isn't Pure Intimacy's oil, but your ass is just too beautiful for me not to massage it." He said.
I chuckled and bent over the ottoman with my ass in the air to give him full access. He held the bottle in the air and let the oil drizzle all over my backside. His large, rough hands felt great massaging me. After he was done, he reached for another condom and dropped that dick off right in my tight little pussy.
"Yes. Fuck me just like that and you better not stop." I growled. I stared at him through the mirror and tears welled up in my eyes. This was good. So good. He had found my g-spot and he pounded it like a hammer hitting a nail. I needed this. Yes I had come all this way to suck his dick but baby, I would've done anything just to have this moment. He pulled out and his dick started getting soft. Now what the fuck?! Here my pussy is leaking, I mean dripping wet and his dick is...SOFT??? I wondered if it was just me in the moment. Was he somewhere else mentally? Maybe he didn't want to fuck me.

"Come suck my dick." He said.
I jumped up and grabbed the pillow that was previously on the floor. Terrance sat down on the couch, and I went to work. I wasn't upset but now I was in my head about it. "What's happening right now?" "Is he not present?" "Is my head and pussy tras...?" Nahhhhh. I'm a beast. I understand that all men aren't the same and different men enjoy different things but hell no, it can't be me, can it? I don't know but once Terrance told me that he wasn't going to cum, I wiped my mouth and stood to my feet.

As I slipped back into my dress, he told me how much he enjoyed his time with me, but I wasn't interested in hearing it. He hit me with the "I have to get up early for work" speech and although I didn't doubt that he had to, you never have to tell me twice. I grabbed my things, hugged him, and left.

A couple days later, I was reminded that he was having a play party in Brooklyn, and I thought to myself, "Maybe I should go." Not specifically for him but to network. You never know who will be at these parties and I wanted to fully immerse myself into the culture for my benefit. Maybe a potential business offer will be made, or I'd get more clients for my next tour. I was already on the road heading back to Charlotte from Baltimore, when I made the decision to bust a U-turn in the middle of a road in West Virginia to head back to Baltimore. I immediately went straight to my favorite hoochie mama mall to find an outfit. Once I was done shopping, I left, and went straight to my mom's house to get ready. While shaving my legs, I realized just how crazy I was. I was already two hours into my drive home, turned around just to drive those same two hours back to Maryland then planned to drive three more hours to Brooklyn just for a party that lasted four to five hours. Yep, crazy as hell indeed.

My makeup was perfect, dress was perfect, shoes were perfect, now it was time for me to get on the road. I turned on my 'Sensually Yours' playlist to get me in the mood. The event called for sexy and seductive, and I was bringing it. I pulled up to the location at exactly 10PM but I still had to find a parking. No one gets to a party on time, so I drove around, scoping the neighborhood then found a spot right on the corner of the block. I sat in my car awhile then headed into the event at 10:30. As I walked in, his same assistant from a couple days ago, greeted me with a hug. As she gave me the instructions for the evening, Terrance walked up the stairs and stopped dead in his tracks when he saw me. I mean, I knew he would. I wore a black, short, netted dress, almost like a bikini coverup, that had a deep V down the front and back. My 7-inch black strappy sandal stilettos were the star of the show, though. My skin was glistening, and I smelled delicious. He finally opened his mouth to speak.

"Wow. You look amazing." He said, as he came in for a hug. "You smell even more amazing, damn Dash." He whispered in my ear.

Everything I do is done with intention and grace so, I knew I'd get compliments all evening. I went down the stairs to where the party would be held and was met by a host of beautiful people. Some coming up to me, telling me that they already knew who I was and some not being able to wrap their head around just how beautiful I was in person. It felt great. I was the center of attention at someone else's party. I mean, this wasn't new to me, but I'm always flattered when complimented.

As the party began, the hosts went over the rules for the space and made sure to remind us that consent and safety are the only ways to indulge in one another. I mingled with the attendees and made my way to the bar where I stayed for most of the evening. I had no intentions of playing with anyone, I just wanted to be a voyeur. I watched Terrance from a distance, play with women and enjoy himself but to me, it was a bit lackluster and routined, the same energy I got from him a couple nights ago. "So maybe I wasn't the problem the other night. Maybe it's just... him." I thought. The women were fangirling over him though. They were literally lined up for a piece of him! I giggled to myself and moved to another spot for a closer look. I was intrigued, yes, but not turned on. He wasn't fucking them himself but using a fucking machine to do his dirty work. Between women, he walked up to me.

"Are you okay?" he asked. "Are you enjoying yourself?"

"I am. I'm enjoying seeing you do your thing." I responded. "Are you playing tonight?" he inquired. "I'm not. I'm just watching. I'm working and doing some research." I joked. "The only way I'll play is if you let me have a round two. I feel like something was off when I had you to myself and I can't quite put my finger on it."

We talked for a moment, and he explained exactly what the issue was.

"I thought I wanted throat, esophagus even but that shit is mad uncomfortable." He spoke. "It's like my dick was bending in your throat and it honestly kinda hurt!"

"Why didn't you tell me?!" I questioned. "When we discussed boundaries, that was a way of creating a safe space for the both of us. If at any point you were uncomfortable or in pain, you should've told me otherwise, I wouldn't know. Especially when you're encouraging me to keep doing it."

My voice was soft yet concerned. I wanted him to enjoy me just as I wanted to enjoy him, but I couldn't because I knew he wasn't in the moment with me.

"I dunno." He said, in a very childlike manner. "I just wanted to please you. I didn't want you to feel less than if I brought up the conversation in the moment."

"Terrance, I appreciate you for wanting to spare my feelings, thank you, but that would've been the perfect time to have the conversation. I don't know when we'll see each other again or even if we'll be intimate again. Communicate with me because I'll never know if something is wrong if you don't." He agreed and gave me a hug.

"You're not mad at me, are you?" He asked. "Not at all."

As the night progressed, I mingled and ended up back at the bar. I probably drank a little too much. So much, that the owners of the space offered me a comfortable place to sleep for the night. Now, I wasn't drunk, just a little tipsy but still fully aware of my surroundings. I probably should've stayed just to be safe though. I didn't. I went to my car, kicked off my shoes and drove to my friend's house in Philly.

All was well until a couple weeks later; he dropped a podcast episode speaking about his experience and how he thought he wanted throat. I didn't listen to the entire thing,
just a snippet. That and the comments were enough for me to speak my peace, no spellcheck.
"Did you tell her that you were uncomfortable while she was sucking your dick, or did you encourage her to keep going???" I typed in the comment section. Now of course, no one knew it was me that he was

talking about in the clip, but I still had to make my presence known. Although I knew he'd make a podcast episode about it, I didn't like the way he tried to joke about it as if he made it clear to me that he was uncomfortable in that moment. The minute my comment posted; Terrance called me. "Yoooo! You're not tight, are you?" he asked.

"Hey Terrance! No, I'm not upset at all! You spoke about your experience and so did I."

"Wait, you spoke about your experience? With me? Where??" He questioned.

Terrance's platform may be larger than mine but once I finally got back home from Brooklyn, I decided to do a story time on Patreon for my followers. Once his episode dropped, my dm's were flooded with people putting two and two together! I thought the shit was hilarious. Especially because they were so curious. I didn't confirm or deny anything, I just watched them try to put the pieces of the puzzle together.

"I did a story time about our encounter on Patreon." I said to him.

Terrance laughed and asked me to send him the video. I told him I would and hung up the phone but not before telling him that he needs to learn how to communicate his intimate boundaries better. Whether it be with me or another woman, communication is a large key to any kind of relationship.

I haven't really talked to Terrance since then. I did send him some merch from my apparel line though. We're cool. There aren't any issues. Things seem to have gone back to the way they were three years ago, when we'd just communicate through social media. I'll like something he post; he may do the same in return but that's just it. What has me cracking up as I type this, is y'all know exactly who I'm talking about!

Dash

JOHN

Remember John? If you don't, allow me to give you a quick reminder. John was another one of my clients in 2023 while I was on tour in New Jersey. Now, you may think to yourself, "Does she fuck all her clients?" I absolutely do...not! Just a few. Just the ones I WANT to fuck, with consent of course! Anyway, I was supposed to meet him a year prior when a woman he was dating, booked me for a couples massage. Leading up to the day, she asked if she could modify the appointment and book the two hours for herself instead of a couples massage. I had no objections, especially since she had already paid in full but, I still wanted to know what happened between them. Apparently, he had pissed her off so bad, that she broke up with him and used that time with me, to pour into herself. I already had his photo, name and contact information from when she inquired, so when he reached out to book the same appointment she had, I knew exactly who he was. Unfortunately, at that time, I was already completely booked and couldn't accommodate him. I assume he kept up with my tour schedule because when I circled back to New Jersey the following year, he made the cut.

I sent John the instructions to the room and as he approached the door, I slowly opened it. The room was dark but the lighting from the candles placed strategically throughout the room, made it a dimly lit, romantic setting. John walked in the room, and I wasn't expecting him to be as big as he was. He stood at about 6'5, hell, he was probably taller than that! The smell of his cologne tickled my nose as I closed the door behind him.
"Welcome in." I spoke softly.
He looked just like his picture and the only two things my eyes locked in on, were his big ass lips and his big ass arms. He looked like he could easily bench press all 180 pounds of me and I kinda wanted to find out. I didn't waste any time, so I went over my disclaimer, as I do with every client, and got to work. I went through the motions and John couldn't keep his eyes off me. It can be a bit weird to be massaging someone and they're just giving you the death stare the entire time, but I like to use it to my advantage. I've been told that I have really seductive eyes so putting clients under my spell wasn't a problem. I'm very intentional with my outfits while massaging men so I wasn't surprised by his eyes dancing over my body. I wore an all-black, all lace teddy that accentuated my figure.

The entire back of the teddy was cut out so when his fingers grazed across my back, all I felt were chills which in turn, made my pussy throb.

I finished up his massage and began cleaning up. John grabbed me by my arm, unexpectedly pulling me in for a hug, and just held me. We swayed back and forth for a while, and it felt good to be in his arms. It felt safe. I was comfortable there, in the embrace of a complete stranger. I hugged him back as I buried my face damn near in his arm pit. John stood towering over my 5'5 frame and honestly, I didn't want him to let me go. If I could've stay in his arms all evening, I would've but I had another client after him. A client I was looking froward to seeing. "Why don't you let me come back and show you a good time tonight?" John whispered in my ear.

It sounded good and his embrace felt nice, and I was craving the attention, but I just wasn't in the mood. "I'm on my period and I'm sure I won't be up to entertaining after a long day of clients." I said.

That didn't seem to faze him at all because his rebuttal was, "That's cool, we can just cuddle." I knew what that was code for. He run red lights. But also, I don't like when someone try to force themselves on me. I went with it because I really needed him out of the room so I can shower and prepare for my next client.

My next client, Casper, came and I was so excited to massage him. Just from his photo alone, I knew I'd have a good time with him. We talked for a moment after his service and it wasn't until he was gone, that he texted and asked me out to dinner. I wanted more time with him, so I obliged. I went to dinner with Casper after cleaning up for the day, and my phone would not stop vibrating the entire time! Although it was on silent, Casper could see the slight irritation on my face.

"If you need to get that, I understand."

"No, it's fine." I responded. "It can wait."

Casper excused himself to the restroom a few minutes later which gave me a small window to check my phone. It was John. Blowing up my phone back to fucking back! I had already told him that I would be busy until 10PM so the back-to-back phone calls and texts was overkill. As I read the messages, he was expressing to me that he cancelled his prior engagements and was waiting for me in the hotel lobby. Uhm, sir! You don't think that's a bit stalker-ish?? Apparently not but just as I started to reply, Casper reappeared at the table. We finished up dinner and he dropped me back to my hotel.

As I entered through the sliding doors, John was sitting there watching me. Had he just seen me hugged up with Casper a moment ago? Did he see the kiss we shared?? Honestly, I didn't care. I had no ties to either of them plus, I was single! "Hey!" I exclaimed. "Are you ready to head upstairs?"

"I am." His voice was low, lower than earlier. I couldn't put my finger on if it was irritation or just him being tired. I didn't ask. I led the way to the elevators, and we rode it floor by floor in silence.

We reached my room and once inside, I walked swiftly to the shower. Once out, I popped in a tampon, put on a pair of silk baby pink booty shorts and a black bralette. I laced my skin with Rosè Body Butter and layered it with Seduction perfume, both by Pure Intimacy. I walked out into the room prepared to climb into bed when I noticed that John sitting on the edge of the bed, with his clothes off. Although his boxers were still on, I wondered what happened to just cuddling?? We both got into bed, and I threw my leg over him prompting him to grab my ass. He did just that. We laid there for a moment in silence. I didn't have anything to say. I was tired and really wanted to sleep, especially after a long day of clients, but my left titty had other plans. It popped out of my bra and expeditiously, John popped it into his mouth. Now, my left nipple is the one you want to go after if you're trying to get something started. It's a direct connection to my clit. No, he didn't know that, and I was too weak in the knees to tell him to stop. He sucked my nipple just right. I mean, his tongue was swirling all around, hitting every single angle. "Sttttt.." I couldn't get the damn word out of my mouth. Have you ever experienced a nipple orgasm? Your nipples being stimulated to the point of explosion??? He adjusted himself to now being on top of me. He cupped both breasts in both hands and went back and forth, showing them the same amount of attention. He then squeezed them together and sucked both nipples AT THE SAME DAMN TIME!!!

"Fuuuckkk! Wh-attt happened to just cccudl-inggg?" I managed to ask through moans.
"If you want me to stop, say it." He shot back.
I wasn't going to say that because I didn't want him to. It felt so damn good. John sucked and licked on

my nipples for maybe 20 minutes. Yes, 20 minutes and no, I'm not exaggerating. He teased me so much, that I feared the bed would have a big red puddle once I got up. He began to kiss down my belly and we were now at the point of no return.

"Did you forget that I'm on my period?" I asked softly, trying to play coy.
"Baby, I'm a grown ass man."
Just that statement alone had me lifting up off the bed for him to pull my shorts off. John pulled my tampon string to the side and went in for the kill. He kissed my clit, over and over and over until I squirmed on the bed. I reached down to hold both sides of his face. I wanted my pussy in his mouth right now, but he shook his head no.

"I'll eat you when I'm ready. Right now, I wanted to give this big ass clit the kisses she's been missing." John said.
Baby, did you clutch your invisible pearls the same way I did? The chills shot down my spine just typing it. My hands returned back to resting on his arms and I got lost in the moment. I was so turned on. John then gripped me by the waist and lifted me slightly off the bed. He licked me from the top of my ass crack all the way back to my clit. I let out a loud moan then suddenly, he tongue-kissed my pearl. I mean slowly. In the same ways he swirled his tongue on my nipples but this time, with more power. He'd go from flickering motions to sucking, to spelling out the alphabet. His tongue pressed down on my clit, and he didn't move it. I massaged my nipple and grinded myself into his mouth. I reached for his head again, this time, I was cumming, IN HIS MOUTH.

"Your mouth feel so good on my fucking pussy." I moaned John finally came up for air but just stared at my pussy.

"Look at that big clit just staring back at me. I think she's asking for more."

Before my body could even catch up and before I could respond to him, he started eating my pussy again. You know how after an intense orgasm; you need time to collect yourself? Your body is still going through spasms and your clit is swollen? I wasn't given that time and I thought I'd need it but, no. My body didn't need rest. It didn't need time to catch up. I wasn't fragile. Or maybe I was but he was so masterful in his eating that I didn't notice. John swallowed up my entire pussy, I mean lips and everything. Sucking gently, I knew I was on the brink of orgasm again, but I wanted to see if I could edge myself. I didn't want the sensations to end. His hands had now replaced mine as he massaged my nipples with his thumb and index finger. Occasionally, he'd squeeze them then back to massaging them. He never stopped tongue kissing my pussy.

"Yes! Yes! Yes!!! Right there! OMG!!!" I screamed. I didn't care about anyone hearing me. I've had good head before but never like this.

"Let this pretty pussy cum in my mouth again." He said.

I followed his clear and concise instructions as I let go for the second time. Edging where? Edging who??? I forgot what the damn word meant. I came, but still, he didn't stop. John was thorough in his eating. Every way his tongue went, my body followed. With our fingers interlocked, he pinned me to the bed. I tried to run because I just couldn't handle it anymore, but he had me locked in. This orgasm was going to be different from the first two. You ever been bound, even with just their hands and the mere thought of being stuck in that position made your pussy throb? That's where I was. The strength he possessed was unfathomable. This go 'round, John slowed his pace even more. Now this, tortured me. I wanted to cum, and I knew he'd let me if I asked.

"John." My voice a whisper. "Please."
"Please what?"
"Please, can I cum. I want to cum." I cried out.
"Were you thinking about cumming when you kissed the other guy earlier??"

I was silent because WHATTTTT???????
"Answer me." His voice was stern.
"No." I said. He kept eating.
Why was he questioning me on something that had nothing to do with him? But honestly, I was even more turned on because the slight jealousy was sexy.

"This pussy is mine and your mouth is mine. I better never see you give it away again. Do you understand?"
Once again, I didn't respond.
"Do you understand?" John asked again.

I knew my silence could lead to one of two things. He'd stop eating my pussy and not let me cum or he'd devour me, and I'd be left shaking on the bed. Of course, I wanted the second option so me being the brat that I am, ignored his question. Just as I suspected, he released my fingers, held my legs up above my head with one hand and fingered my asshole with the other. That man ate my pussycat off the bone until I was dripping in his mouth! I had never and I do mean NEVER experienced a climax like that before. Three clitoral orgasms back-to-back??? The man knew my body better than I did. John sat up on the bed, looked at me with a smile on his face and said, "Do you understand?"

"Yes, I understand."

I hurried to the restroom to shower, again. Thankfully, there were no big red puddles on the bed. When I made it back to him nice and fresh, the only words John uttered were "Sit on my face, right now." Goddammit!!! I need a break! My pussycat was still trying to recover and all he could think about was more pussy?!
"You don't think I need a break?" I wept.
"No." he said. "Sit on my face."
I dropped the towel and crawled onto his face. John ate my pussy well into the night, over and over again. The next day, I could barely walk straight from my clit being so swollen.

To this day, we still keep in contact. Any time I'm in his neck of the woods, I call him because I want that same treatment as before. The last time I saw John, he was recovering from an operation, and I was walking around his place, in his t-shirt, catering to him until a knock on the door scared the hell out of me. He encouraged me to open it and on the other side, stood his adult daughter and his granddaughter. Here I am, already embarrassed to be answering his door but to answer his door in nothing but a t-shirt for his DAUGHTER!! HIS ADULT DAUGHTER! I finished making his food then got in the bed with the blanket pulled over my head. She came into the room, and they talked for what felt like an eternity. Meanwhile, I couldn't wait to get dressed and leave.

He finished his food and asked if I could return his plate to the kitchen. I did and as I came back to the room, he was returning from the bathroom.I pulled the shirt over my head to put my own clothes back on. "Where are you going? What's wrong?" he questioned.

I couldn't hide my irritation and after explaining what the issue was, he just wasn't seeing my point. "Dash, take your clothes off and get back in the bed." "No."

Now it wasn't a hard no, but I really was uncomfortable having sex with him now that his daughter and granddaughter were home. I could hear the baby girl calling for her 'Pop-pop' from the basement.

"Dash, please take your clothes off and get back in bed. I won't ask you again." He spoke.
I didn't listen to him. At this point, I was completely dressed and ready to head out. He didn't have much mobility being that he was fresh off the operation table, but the man grabbed my arm, pushed me down on the bed, hiked up my little black dress and started eating my pussy, WITH THE BEDROOM DOOR WIDE THE FUCK OPEN!

Dash

LEO

Let's chat about Leo. Leo to this day, is such a phenomenal man. I met him 7 years ago at a club in DC after one of my girlfriends called me up asking if I wanted to go out. I'm not a party girl at all but I do like to step out occasionally, so I locked in a babysitter, my mom, and told her yes. I quickly got dressed and drove to her house. It didn't make sense to take multiple cars, so after picking up a few of her friends, we got on the road to DC. This was my first time experiencing DC nightlife and as much as I wanted to enjoy it, I wasn't 100% present. I was a new mom so being away from my baby for an extended period of time, just didn't feel right. Plus, I wished I drove because when I'm ready to go, I'm ready to go!

We pulled up to the club and the line was already crazy long. We hopped out, valeted the car, and stood in line, waiting our turn to enter. Finally, inside, me and my girls took off to the ladies room; that's always the first stop to freshen up. I allowed them to walk in front of me, taking on that mama/bodyguard role. As we excused ourselves through the crowd, the world seemed to stop as I walked pass this man who had an exceptional, charismatic air about him. This man was created and came straight from God himself. We locked eyes and I drunk in every bit of him. He was six feet tall and light in complexion with salt and pepper locs that hung down his back and a beard to match. He wore black specs that framed his face perfectly. Leo wore an all-black, well-tailored suit and a white button up shirt and a black tie. His look was simple yet classic. My friends pulled me out of my gaze as we hurried off to the ladies' room.

Back out into the crowd, I noticed Leo again. I mean, he was pretty hard to miss. The presence that radiated off this man, was like none other. He caught me staring at him and stopped me in my tracks. "Hello beautiful." He spoke. "How are you?" The cadence in which he spoke, the tone of his voice combined with his thick DC accent, gave me a chill. "Hello handsome. I'm well, thank you. How are you?" With the music blaring so loud, we could barely hear each other. He grabbed me by my waist, pulling me into him. Throwing my arms up over his shoulders, I eagerly listened to every word he said. Our interaction felt so natural. Almost as if we had known each other for some time.

"So, I take it that you're single?" I questioned.

I knew that he had to be the way he grabbed me up and began speaking sweet nothings in my ear.

"No, I'm not. I'm actually married."

Of course, he's married! Apart of me felt a little crushed but the other half didn't care at all. He vaguely explained his marital status, the typical, we're separated, blah blah blah. I made up my mind right then, that I was going to keep him around. Call me crazy, shit, call me a homewrecker, but if he didn't care, neither did I. Leo and I exchanged numbers and continued flirting throughout the night. He was actually the head security guard at the club. He guarded me and my friends the entire night and made sure we had a good time. How we ended up having our own section in the club, I don't know but thank you Leo!

We communicated a lot throughout the next few weeks. I would go to the club almost every weekend by myself just to spend time with him. His club became my "mommy free" time. We've had a few encounters but none like the one a few years ago. I was home on leave from the army for Christmas and my first night, I just knew where I was going, DC. I called up my girls and of course they were ready to help me celebrate my short time home. I made my twin brother come also because although Leo would've made sure we were okay; I wanted my own personal driver and bodyguard. We pulled up and did the usual, valeted the car and got in line. This particular night, we got in the express line. It was cold as hell outside, and I didn't feel like waiting. Once inside, the ladies and I walked straight to the restroom while my brother ordered our drinks. We partied the night away and of course, me and Leo were all over each other. It didn't matter that he was working. He'd hang out with me then go do his rounds. Before leaving the club, Leo and I agreed to link up that coming Tuesday, Christmas Eve.

I took the hour drive from Baltimore to DC early Tuesday morning. I was excited to spend the entire day with him. I checked into the hotel and waited.
"I'm downstairs." He texted.

The hotel required a key card to gain access, so I slipped on some sweats and went to meet him in the lobby. Leo is very known in DC so in public, we couldn't do too much but in private??? Well... Once on the elevator, we could barely keep our hands to ourselves. Leo pulled me into him, spreading his fingers across my ass then squeezing it. I felt his dick jump through his jeans and I couldn't wait to have it inside of me. We got to the room, and I stripped down to my birthday suit and wrapped myself in one of the hotel robes.

Leo was undressing to take a shower but before I let him off to the bathroom, I had to taste that dick of his.
"Come here." I said to him, while simultaneously motioning him with my finger. I laid on my stomach while Leo walked over to the side of the bed. I went to work, my head bobbing like the pro that I am.

"Damn, I miss this mouth." He moaned.

I looked up at him, smiled then swallowed him. He lost it. After about a minute or two, I stopped and repositioned myself on the full, fluffy pillows behind me.

"That's all you get." I said. "Go shower. I'm not going anywhere."

"You're gonna send me away with my dick leaking like this?"

I didn't respond. I just looked at him with a very mischievous smile.

Out of the shower, Leo glided across the hotel room floor, making a beeline straight to me. No words were spoken between either of us, just eye contact. He climbed onto the bed, spread my legs, and started feasting as if it was the last supper.

"Damn baby, just like that." I spoke softly.

He ate my pussy with precision. I grabbed a handful of his locs and gently tugged at them. The shit felt amazing! He was so meticulous with his movements. Every time I tried to run from his mouth, he'd follow me up the bed.

"Leo! Fuck!" I exclaimed. "Your mouth feels so good on my pussy."

"Mhmm." He groaned, never lifting his head.

I knew that he wanted my juices all over his face. We had a lasting joke that every time he saw me, he wanted me to moisturize his beard and face, anytime, anyplace.

"Leo, please." I begged.

The pressure from his tongue flicking across my clit then sucking it, sent me over the edge. I couldn't hold it any longer. As my body began shaking uncontrollably, he dug his fingers into my skin, and held me still.

"Fuck! Leo, I'm cumming!!! I yelled.

My body jerked as I came down off my high. Leo crawled up on top of me and allowed me to taste myself, the remaining juices that rested on his lips and tongue. He leaned back on his knees, spread my legs as far as the could go, one ankle in each hand, and admired my body.

Leo used his body to guide his dick to my center and slowly slid into me. After four months of absolutely no sexual activity, my body was sensitive to every little touch. I let out a loud, long sigh at the pleasurable feeling of Leo's dick deep inside of me. He watched me closely and I, him. We never took our eyes off each other, not for one second. He catered to my body's every need. Every move he made; I matched it. Every moan, he countered it. Leo had me reaching for shit that wasn't even there! I wanted to talk my shit, but I couldn't. he had full control over my body. He gripped my ankles and rolled me over to my stomach. He grabbed my hips, raised me up off the bed and went in. He fucked me hard until I collapsed. Panting. No one has EVER made me tap out before and I wasn't about to let it happen.

"I want to ride your dick." I whispered.

I didn't wait for his response; I just mounted him. Already on the tips of my toes, I placed my hands on his chest for balance. He grabbed my ass and spread my cheeks for more access. As I came down on him, he thrusted upwards into me. Hard. I wanted all of his dick and here I was, taking it. My entire body shivered with pleasure. I continued bouncing up and down on him. His eyes damn near rolled to the back of his head. I leaned down on him, wrapping my arms around his neck and tucking my legs and feet under his. I had him locked in now. I twerked on the tip then dropped down causing him to let out a loud moan. I did it over and over again. I missed him and I wanted him to know just how much.

We went at it all damn day. Fucking each other like two horny rabbits. I didn't want to leave him, but I knew our time together was coming to an end. I pulled Leo into the bathroom, bent over the counter, looked at him through the mirror and demanded that he fuck me.
"Oh yeah, that's how you want it?"
"This is exactly how I want it." I replied.
Using the last bit of energy we had, Leo grabbed my neck with both hands and fucked me hard. We watched each other in the mirror, and I couldn't help but notice the tears streaming down my cheeks. Not because I was in pain, but the pressure that was built up and him knocking down every wall I had, made me emotional. The passion was there. My pleasure was prioritized. I can't explain the feeling I felt or even what I'm feeling now as I write this. He was so aggressive with me. Aggressive yet gentle. My juices were running down my legs and I didn't want him to stop. He switched up his tempo and started slow stroking me. Every time he reentered me, he would slam into me, forcing all 9 inches of dick in me. I gasped for air each time. My moans were more of a whisper. He fucked me until we both came, him in me, and watched each other while doing so.

As we showered together, I slowly floated down from cloud 9. I relished in the last few moments we had left. I knew that it would be a while before I saw him again. We snuggled and made out before heading out to my car. We talked for about an hour, until we could no longer prolong the time. It's okay though. I know exactly where to find him when I need him.

Dash

JOSH

I fucked a pornstar! Or should I say that a pornstar fucked me?? Because I never experienced the subspace until he had me slightly bent over my massage table with his hands firmly gripping my neck. I love him. Lmao! I love him. Josh is my man that's not my man but absolutely IS my man! I meet a lot of people on social media, and Josh is no different.

Scrolling on twitter one day, a video of him fucking a gorgeous, bald petite woman popped up. Intrigued, I went to his page. Man oh man. Josh was tall, 6'5, chocolate as hell, bald and bearded, just like I like them. His body was perfect, so perfect that I'd lick the sweat that cascaded down his abs. I sent him a message right then because why wait?

"Put that dick in my throat Papa." I typed. There was no need to be subtle. I knew what I wanted, and I was going for it. Needless to say, he never responded, not until sometime later, at least. Josh had retweeted one of my videos where I was giving a woman a sensual nuru massage. It was only a 5 second snippet but it showed a lot. Not only did he retweet it, but he also followed me. I took that as my opportunity to message him again. This time, I had a different approach.

"Good afternoon. My name is Dash and I'm a sensual masseuse. I love your content! What I'd love more, is to have you on my table with my hands and body all over you." After I sent the message, I logged off Twitter. To my surprise, he messaged me back pretty quickly. We exchanged pleasantries, and he agreed to a massage but only if we could record it. Hell yes, we can record it! He expressed that not only would he want the video for himself, but it serves as content for both of us. We set up a date and time and exchanged numbers.

It was early April, and I was still celebrating my birthday with a city hopping tour. Josh being in Atlanta just happened to fit into my already scheduled visit. I packed up my things to prepare for my nine-hour drive from Baltimore to Atlanta. I was no stranger to road trips, so fuck it, why not? Once checked into my hotel room, I set up all of my equipment and showered while I waited for Josh to arrive. I noticed that the bathroom sink wasn't draining, so I called the front desk to have them fix the problem. Almost immediately, maintenance was knocking on my door. To my surprise, it was a woman. The moment she began working on the sink, Josh texted me that he was in the lobby, so I sent him the room number. The door to the room was sitting ajar due to the toolbox being there so I saw him approaching the door. He walked up at the tail end of me and the he woman's conversation and heard us giggling.

"What so funny?" He asked.

I had just finished asking the woman if she could come back later because I had a guest coming and when she saw Josh, we both cackled.

"Oh, nothing." I smiled.

She packed up her things and left.

"Hi beautiful, how are you?" He asked.

Damn! He was even finer in person. The sun peaked through the sheer curtains and loved up on his gorgeous skin. Josh reached out to hug me.

"I'm doing good, thank you. Thank you for coming." He smelled so good, really good. Earthy. Kinda like sandalwood and patchouli. Josh wore a loose fitted 'hammertime' jumper with no shirt. I, for obvious reasons, was naked and wrapped in a towel. I explained to him that I would be giving him a nuru massage and thoroughly expressed what it entailed. I absolutely wanted to fuck this man however, we never had that conversation. He was here to get a massage, and I was here to give him one.

Josh set up his camera and we got to work. I was impressed with how relaxed he was. He would caress me as I massaged him, and it felt, nice. His big hands rubbing my backside while I massaged his legs, felt.. nice. When I flipped him over. My eyes went straight to his dick. I wanted to see if it was just as beautiful as his pictures and videos on Twitter. It was big but soft. I went through the motions of his massage, gliding my body up and down his, oil everywhere, doing my signature look into the camera, you know. When I got to his lingam massage, I was kinda upset because his dick never got hard. His massage was ending, and I knew that we had good footage, so I wasn't too upset.

Josh was packing up to leave and although I wanted to fuck him, my nerves got the best of me. Eventually, I gave in.
"Next time, I want to know what that dick feels like."
"Why wait until next time?" He questioned.
"We don't have to."
I stood up and slowly unwrapped the towel. Josh undressed and sat in the chair behind him. I walked up, kneeled between his legs, and started sucking his dick. At first, the entire thing fit in my mouth until it started growing! There. It was the dick from the pictures and videos. Josh's dick was about 12 inches. Big. The biggest dick I've ever had. It was chocolate and thick. His veins protruded out, making it look like the perfect snickers bar. Of course, his dick couldn't fit in my mouth, but that wasn't going to stop me from trying to take all of it. Josh reached for his phone, which turned out to be mine, and recorded me. He guided me on how he wanted me to suck his dick, just the head, lick up the shaft, play with his balls, spit on it, then eat it up. Just the way he instructed me, turned me on. The way he looked at me. The way he bit his lip. He held the phone with one hand, and with the other reached down to smack my ass.

"Goddamn, you're beautiful." He said.

I looked up at him as a tear escaped my eye. Josh wiped it away with his thumb, stood up, placed both hands on the back of my head and fucked my throat. When I reached to brace the blows, he smacked my hands out of the way.

"Nah, I want to feel this throat. Put your fucking hands down." He spoke.

I did as I was told and bound my hands behind my back. Spit dripped out of my mouth as he vigorously massaged my esophagus.

In one swift motion, Josh picked me up and placed me on the bed. He laid on his back and told me to ride him. I didn't know how I was going to take all 12 inches of him, but I did it like a good girl. I climbed up on my feet, grabbed ahold of his neck, and slowly worked every inch inside of me. Josh reached under my legs, gripping my ass to help lower me down onto him. Once all of him was inside of me, we locked eyes, and I just sat there.

"You feel that dick baby?" He question.

"Yessss." I moaned

I threw my head back in pleasure. I know that I can take dick, I've done it plenty of times before. But 12 inches of this thick ass dick? All of it inside of me? This is going to be a wild ride. I began to grind on him, then bouncing up and down. He thrusted upward into me, and I couldn't contain my screams. I adjusted myself so now I'm on my knees, and I laid on top of him. Josh squeezed and hugged me so tight, holding me still while he pounded my pussy over and over again. My arms, wrapped around his neck, I took it. I nestled my face in his neck and took it.

I didn't have time to show him that my momma made a hoe. Josh fucked me senseless, and I had no objections. We rolled over together, dick still inside of me and he continued to pound me. Up on his knees, he covered his face as he slowed his rhythm.

"FUUUUUUCCCCKKKKK." He growled.

His mouth hung open like he had more to say but no words came out. Tell Me by Usher was playing and Josh rocked my boat to the cadence of the song. Slow and steady. He would pull all the way out then put it all back in. The pressure building up in my pussycat, made me want him to dig deep and never let up. I think he could feel that, so he stopped. He climbed off the bed, sat back in the chair, and told me to come suck his dick. I sprung up off the bed and did as I was told. He loved when I gagged on his dick. My face was soaked with tears.

"There you go. Eat that dick just like that." He said.

I massaged his dick with my hands while sucking it simultaneously.

"You gonna make Daddy cum in that pretty like mouth of yours."

"But I don't want Daddy to cum yet." I said, frowning.

A moment passed and you would've thought I was bobblehead the way I slobbed on his knob.

"Get up." He responded.

I got up and bent over my massage table. Josh repositioned the camera behind us then smashed me to smithereens. I propped one leg up on the table to give him better access to me. He grabbed my neck with both hands and squeezed tightly. So tight that I was gasping for air but not crazy tight where I couldn't breathe if that makes sense. He was digging me out. I had zero control. Not of my body or the situation. I was squirting and creaming all over myself and him, but he never stopped fucking me. That's when it happened. My body lost all consciousness. I had heard of the subspace before, but I never experienced it. The subspace is a trance-like euphoria of overtly intense emotions. It's essentially, unlocking ecstasy. You feel it so deep in you, and your entire body just goes limp. You're still present but there's nothing you can do. Your body loses consciousness but just for a quick moment. Three seconds felt more like 3 minutes though with Josh. My pussy throbs just thinking about it. He paid attention to my body because he loosened the grip he had around my neck and slowed his stroke. Him smacking my ass, brought me back to reality, quickly.

"This pussy so good. You're taking Daddy dick like you know what you're doing."

"Fuck me Daddy," I managed to say.

"You want Daddy to fuck you Princess?"

"Yes, please."

I didn't have any energy. My body gave in to pleasure. I was still feeling the remnants of the subspace.

"Open that pussy up for Daddy." He spoke.

I reached back to spread my ass open for him. My face rested in the leather of my massage table, and I just took it. No words, no sound. I just took it. You know the dick is good when you can't even moan. You try to muster up something, but the words fail you.

"Daddy is about to cum baby."

"Cum in my pussy Daddy."

I found the words from somewhere. Josh grabbed my waist and slammed himself into me repeatedly. "Arrgghhhhh!!"
He deposited his load in my pussy and fell back onto the bed. I stayed bent over the table pushing out his nut and the warm sensation dripping down my clit, made me shiver a bit.

I finally stood up, pressed stop on the camera and walked to the bathroom. Josh followed me and we showered together. We were in the shower for what seemed like forever, kissing, and fucking. Once dressed, we talked for a moment, then he left. I sat and watched the video we made, just replaying it in my mind, marveling at how amazing I felt. I wondered how we'd turn an hour and 20 minute masterpiece into 30 minutes of content for our fan pages. I sent him the entire thing and let him make the final edits.

I talk to Josh often and every time I'm in Atlanta, we make art. Personally and professionally. He always get a massage and I'm always freshly fucked, the perfect tradeoff. I like to use Josh as my muse when I have to perform live because my gorgeous chocolate body on his perfect chocolate body completely covered in oil, is a sight to see! Haha.

Dash

OUTRO

You've made it to the end of the book. Give yourself a round of applause! If you're a reader like me, you read this in one day, however I overstand wanting that feeling of pleasure and the need for an element of surprise, to last a bit longer. If that's you, you probably read a chapter a day. First, I appreciate your support! Thank you for buying this book and investing into Pure Intimacy. You don't have to be a client that experienced healing, relaxation and heightened sensual encounters on my table, or even purchased products from me. Just a follow-on social media is an investment into my brand, and it's appreciated, truly. Secondly, this book is a bit of healing for me. Although I have stories I could tell for days, like my visit to a sex dungeon that ended in a threesome or how fucking my mother's friend husband got me a UTI, I'm just not in the space of casual sex anymore. It isn't fulfilling. Writing these chapters helped me realized just how lack luster and boring my pleasure life is. So, although interesting, I long for romance, intimacy, pleasure, intention, effort, and foreplay that last at minimum, 24 hours. You can't get that casually! I've had my fun, Lord knows I have, but I want more. They say you can't turn a hoe into a housewife, but you cannot spell home without the HO! Lmao!!!

My prayer is that you've enjoyed this piece of work. I pray that it provided some laughs and some "action", whether alone or you pulled out the little black book to call up a honey. I had fun writing this. It took a lot of thinking, porn, wine, and late nights to complete it but I did it. I fucking did it! I'm sure you've noticed that some of these chapters happened when I was a lot younger so please don't judge me for my actions or ways of thinking at that time. What they say, 'I was young, dumb and full of cum!'

If you've enjoyed this, leave me a review. Tell me your favorite chapter and part. If you didn't like it, still, leave me a review, a constructive critique! Don't forget, I'm from Baltimore so don't be rude! J/k.

I love you all <3 Thank you! Xo, Dash

Dash

Dash

Dash

Made in the USA
Columbia, SC
10 April 2024

34195646R00072